THE CORRUPTED

THE ⊕ LAST IMMORTAL

By Alex Marlowe

The Last Immortal
The Last Immortal: Soul Hunter
The Last Immortal: The Corrupted

THE CORRUPTED

THE LAST IMMORTAL

alex MARLOWE

LITTLE, BROWN BOOKS FOR YOUNG READERS
www.lbkids.co.uk

LITTLE, BROWN BOOKS FOR YOUNG READERS

First published in Great Britain in 2017 by Hodder and Stoughton

1 3 5 7 9 10 8 6 4 2

Text copyright © Working Partners Ltd, 2017

The moral right of the author has been asserted.

A CIP catalogue record for this book
is available from the British Library.

ISBN 978-0-349131-84-9

Typeset in Caslon by M Rules
Printed and bound in Great Britain
by Clays Ltd, St Ives plc

The paper and board used in this book are
made from wood from responsible sources.

MIX
Paper from
responsible sources
FSC® C104740
FSC
www.fsc.org

Little, Brown Books for Young Readers
An imprint of
Hachette Children's Group
Part of Hodder and Stoughton
Carmelite House
50 Victoria Embankment
London EC4Y 0DZ

An Hachette UK Company
www.hachette.co.uk

www.hachettechildrens.co.uk

To James Moruzzi

With special thanks to Michael Ford

CHAPTER 1

"I can smell that troll from here," muttered Dodger, nudging Luke and nodding towards the crowd of supernatural creatures shuffling into ranks beneath the dais where Luke and Dodger were standing. The funeral was due to start any minute, but shadowy figures were still arriving in the small graveyard overlooked by the moonlit towers of Southwark Cathedral. An empty trestle table stood beside Luke on the dais, awaiting Jonathan Harker's coffin.

"Keep your voice down," said Luke, shooting a glance at the hulking sewer troll in the second row. "And maybe try having some respect."

"Exactly my point," Dodger whispered, removing his top hat and smoothing his greasy hair. "A bath and a spritz of aftershave doesn't hurt anyone."

Luke shook his head. Expecting Dodger to behave with decorum was like expecting Aurora Cage to take up knitting. Most of the time, the street urchin could be relied upon to lighten the mood, but occasionally Luke wished he'd shut up for five minutes.

"Perhaps you should go and check the perimeter again?" Luke said.

Dodger shrugged. "The blood-suckers are on it, aren't they?"

"The roof, then," said Luke, impatiently.

Dodger muttered something about not being Luke's "errand boy", pulled on his hat again, and stalked off among the gravestones and tombs. Luke was glad. The last thing they needed was his Victorian friend offending the guests with his less-than-discreet whispers. Not least when so many of them had short tempers and lethal abilities.

Most of London's supernatural communities had sent representatives for Harker's funeral. A gathering of so many different types of creature in one location was almost unheard of, and Luke could sense the tension simmering just beneath the surface; sideways glances, muttering, awkward shuffles as the guests lined up. At best, many of the creatures would do everything they could to avoid each other. At worst, they had long and bloody feuds dating back to medieval times. If the Victorian street urchin provoked a fight, things could quickly get out of control, and Evelyn would never forgive him. Luke wouldn't blame her. Growing up, Harker had been like an uncle to him and his death had hit him hard. *I still can't believe he's gone.*

As he gazed over the crowd, Luke wished for a moment that he could make notes in his scrapbook, but he pushed the thought away guiltily. The problem was, even though he'd been reanimated for almost three months now, it was all still so *new*. For years when he was a young boy in the 1850s, he'd been fascinated – ok, *obsessed* – by his father's team of supernatural crime-fighters called the Immortals. He'd kept records of all their missions, and done his best to catch glimpses of their strange encounters and adventures. But he'd always been on the outside – kept at a distance. Now he was one of them, he couldn't quite kill off that old curiosity.

Luke sensed a blur to his right and almost let his lightning blade shoot from his arm in response. But it was only Dodger, skidding to a halt.

"All clear," he said. "This place is like Fort Knox. So where's the guest of honour?"

Luke looked at him blankly.

"Harker," Dodger added.

Luke nudged him with an elbow, hard enough for Dodger to wince. "That's not even slightly funny," he said.

Dodger clutched his ribs. "Hey, you're half metal, remember."

Luke checked his watch – the sun would rise in nine minutes. Then a silence fell over the crowd. Evelyn had begun to walk slowly down the aisle between the guests, wearing a black dress and cap with a veil that looked at least a hundred and fifty years old. Luke felt a lump in his throat as he realised it was probably the same mourning outfit she'd worn at the funeral of her mother and brother, back when the Sisters, Dracula's minions, had killed them. Harker and Evelyn had been left alive – if you could call it that – bitten and turned into the creatures of the night that Harker had hunted for so long. Luke couldn't tell if Evelyn was crying beneath the veil. She wasn't the kind to shed tears easily.

Behind her came Raziel and Aurora carrying Harker's coffin – one at the front and one at the back. The werewolf had removed her hat, and her long hair hung loose over her shoulders. Her broad, scarred face was emotionless, looking straight ahead. Raziel, with the coffin resting on his stone shoulder, was staring at the ground. Though it was Victor Frankenstein, Luke's father, who had brought the Immortals together in Victorian times, Luke knew it was Harker, a supernatural like the rest of them, who had acted as the glue. Luke felt his heart flutter with grief. How they would cope without him, he wasn't sure.

Evelyn passed the front row of guests and took her place on the dais, facing out at the crowd with her head bowed. Now Luke saw she was indeed weeping, her shoulders shaking as she sobbed. He wanted to go to her, but he was supposed to be the master of ceremonies. Raziel and Aurora set the open coffin down on the trestle, then joined the front row of the congregation.

Jonathan Harker lay completely still, looking little different from the day he died a week before. He was the first vampire Luke had seen who had died from Blood Deficiency Syndrome. Effectively, his body had starved itself. Though one of the members of Clarence's Vampire Club had done their best to disguise the dark circles and bloodless lips with make-up, there wasn't much he could have done to mask the skeletal, haunted features of the corpse. Harker wore a brown suit, but it hung loosely off his ravaged body. Luke swallowed. He knew that any self-respecting vampire would rather be staked than die such an undignified death.

It was Harker who, with his daughter's help, had developed the science – biological and chemical and technological – to bring Luke back from the dead, according to his father's dying wishes. He had literally saved Luke's life after his father Victor had preserved him. And when it came down to it, Luke and the other Immortals had been unable to return that favour.

"I think you're up," whispered Dodger to Luke. The pickpocket climbed down from the dais, touching Evelyn slightly on the shoulder as he passed and slipped into the front row next to Raziel.

Luke took his cue, and stepped up to the edge of the platform. His hands were shaking a little as he pulled his notes from his pocket, and gazed out over the crowd of guests.

In the front row, he could see two dark-haired women in sombre suits – members of the *Canes Umbrarum*, the secret society of werewolves. There was little clue in looking at them what lurked beneath their human skins, ready to burst forth at the touch of the Full Moon's light. But Luke knew from his research that certain residual features remained, even in human form. Tougher nails, sharper teeth, thicker hair. A sense of smell a hundred times enhanced beyond that of a human.

Behind the werewolves, Luke recognised the slim, balding figure of Professor Tadic, the aloof sorcerer who worked at the British Library. He had always dealt exclusively with Harker, and Luke wondered if he would be as helpful in future, if they needed him again to access some of the Library's obscure occultist texts. There were river sprites also, barely four feet tall with a blueish tinge to their smooth skin, their gills covered by tall collars. And a ghoul, wearing a black cloak, floating just above the ground. Luke couldn't see any of its actual body – did it even have one? – but its eyes glowed a sickly yellow under its hood.

Of course, by far the majority of the guests were vampires, just like the deceased. At least twenty by a rough count, all dressed from head to toe in black, with hats and high collars and gloves. The only skin showing was their faces, and these were even paler than usual, since they wore high factor UV blocker. It wasn't a myth about vampires and sunlight, but it was exaggerated. They'd evolved over time, so although prolonged exposure to intense sunlight could kill, a few minutes in weak light would more likely produce a very bad case of sunburn. Holy water, garlic and crosses were nonsense. The best way to dispatch *homo vampyricus* was still the old-fashioned one. A sharp stake to the heart, or decapitation.

"Thank you all for coming to pay your respects," said Luke. His voice sounded loud in the silent graveyard, though in the background London's traffic was already rumbling. "Jonathan Harker would have been heartened to see so many of you here today." He looked across the crowd, trying to keep his voice clear and steady. "He was my father's oldest friend and his most trusted. And to Jonathan Harker I owe my ... "

The words tailed off in his mouth, as his eyes fell on a figure standing slightly distant from the rear of the gathering, leaning against a buttress of the cathedral. He was seven feet tall at least, wearing simple clothes – a thick padded shirt of rough undyed cloth. But that wasn't what had drawn Luke's attention. The figure was wearing a battered bronze mask, leaving openings only for his eyes. Luke squinted. He could have sworn he'd seen the mask before, or something very like it, but he couldn't remember where. The man's eyes were fixed on him with curious intensity.

Dodger cleared his throat, and Luke snapped to attention. The guests were all watching him expectantly, waiting for him to continue. He glanced down once more at the paper in his hand.

"Erm, I was saying ... he was my father's trusted friend and I owe my life to him. In many ways, so do we all, for at the head of the Immortals he has kept us safe from countless dangers, over the centuries. I would like to invite his daughter Evelyn Harker to speak – she is the one who knew him best."

Luke gave a small bow and offered his hand to Evelyn as she stepped to the front. She wore black gloves, and squeezed his hand lightly. Luke moved to one side, and saw her tear-stained face as she lifted up her veil. The sun had risen, making the sky pale and windows of the skyscrapers to the east glow gold, but it hadn't yet breached the raised road of London Bridge and the graveyard remained in shadow.

"My father was not a willing vampire," said Evelyn, quietly, "but few of us are. It is a curse that is thrust upon us." A few nods in the crowd. All eyes were on Evelyn. But as Luke glanced again at the masked figure, he saw that the stranger was still watching him. *Who is he? Why is he looking at me?* He tried again to place where he had seen the mask before, but the memory drifted just out of reach.

"At first he despaired," Evelyn continued, "for he had become the thing he hated most. He had shown great courage in travelling to Transylvania to kill the tyrant Dracula, but he paid the price for that bravery with the death of my mother and brother, Quincey. In time he accepted his fate. He was a determined, resourceful man. He made up his mind that if he was to live forever, he would use his time to benefit humanity rather than simply leech off its blood."

Luke sensed the crowd's mood shifting a little at that. Evelyn was treading a fine line between praising her father and offending the vampires in attendance. The masked man kept watching Luke, as still as a statue. It was disconcerting, and Luke made up his mind that he would find him afterwards. Not to confront or accuse – just to find out who he was and ask him about the mask.

Evelyn continued. "Jonathan Harker spent the best part of two centuries fighting evil. He was alone in meeting with all the supernatural communities of London. He always encouraged peace and reconciliation between them. He gave valuable counsel to all of you, and I hope you heed it even after his death. I will remember him as a kind, loving – and sometimes bossy – father." Light laughter, and Luke smiled too. "He never lost his fighting spirit, even at the very end," Evelyn continued after a pause.

Luke could hear that she was struggling to keep the choke out of her voice, so he moved closer to her, ready to take over if need be. She shook her head and waved him off with a small gesture.

"He will never be forgotten. We will miss him greatly," she finished. Then she turned eastwards, and Luke sensed the coming sun. As if on cue, the rays crept around the side of the Shard, illuminating the great glass skyscraper. Golden light flooded the graveyard, lighting up the arches of stained glass in the cathedral's windows. The vampires turned away as one, including Evelyn, but the sun fell upon Harker's exposed body. It began to smoke. Flames caught hold, bright orange but oddly heatless and smokeless. Luke averted his eyes.

The fire lasted only a minute or two. As the flames died, Luke saw that the coffin had remained virtually intact, but Harker's body was gone, leaving only a faint coating of ash. Evelyn was weeping again. Luke felt deep, shuddering emotion welling up inside him. *That's it. He's gone.*

Remembering it was time to end the ceremony, he gathered himself and stepped forward. He thanked the guests, and as he did so, his eyes lingered on the masked man. The stranger had remained where he was, eyes still locked on Luke. Luke ended by directing the crowd to Clarence's Vampire Club for the wake.

As the guests began to break apart, chatting in low tones amongst themselves, Luke was about to push towards the bronze-masked man, when one of the suited werewolves came up to the front, others queuing up behind her to offer their condolences. The werewolf held out a hand to Evelyn, who took it. "My name is Amelie," she said. "Head of the *Canes Umbrarum*." Her accent was cut-glass English aristocracy. "I'm sorry for your loss. Dear Jonathan helped our society many times over the decades. He really was a trusted friend. Please, when your period of mourning is over, come and see us. We must make sure that werewolves and vampires remain on good terms."

"Of course," Evelyn replied, nodding politely.

Next came the ghoul, drifting forwards. His eyes blazed briefly as he spoke in a rasping voice. He told Evelyn that grief was a friend who clung close until the day it was suddenly absent. Luke wasn't sure if the speech was supposed to be comforting or not.

The river sprites and the sorcerer were both waiting in line but it was an elderly vampire who came up next. His eyes were a piercing black, his dark hair in a widow's peak. He wore a navy suit which looked turn of the twentieth century. He kissed Evelyn's gloved hand. "Your father was one of a kind," he said. "We'll miss him at Clarence's, but you are always welcome there, even with your ..." he cast a haughty glance at Luke and Dodger – "... friends."

Luke tried not to be offended. Vampires were notoriously superior.

"Thank you," said Evelyn.

"I assume," the vampire continued in a firmer voice, "that Jonathan's death will mean the disbanding of the Immortals."

It took a moment for the words to register with Luke, and Evelyn's eyes widened in surprise. She opened her mouth to speak but Luke butted in.

"No!" he said, shaking his head.

The vampire hadn't even been looking at him, but turned now, showing his fangs over his bottom lip in a smile that conveyed no warmth.

"What he means," said Evelyn, placing a hand on the vampire's arm, "is, why would we disband? My father would never have wanted that."

The vampire looked left and right, as if checking for anyone who might overhear. "I understand what you are saying, but you should know. Your recent exploits have drawn attention, not just among the supernatural elements of society, but with humans too, even in the United States."

Luke guessed he was talking about the battle against the Soul Hunter, Draka, in Louisiana.

"If we hadn't taken on Draka, you wouldn't be here now," said Luke, interrupting again.

Another cold smile. "There was also an incident with

a helicopter," said the vampire. "Right here over the city. And the partial destruction of a museum in Austria." Luke felt his face redden, much to his annoyance. "We've even had a young journalist accosting our reception staff at the Club. That is quite unaccept—"

"Listen, me old mucker," said Dodger, wandering over. "We don't go about tellin' you which necks to chomp on, so why don't you keep your beak out of our business? Everything we've done was to save innocent lives. So take your pasty features and scarper back to your glass of O Neg at Clarence's."

The vampire, and others close to him, stiffened, and Luke knew they were close to losing their tempers.

"No one asked for your opinion, urchin," said the vampire. "And I'd counsel you to keep your peace, unless you want us to test your immortality the painful way."

Aurora, Luke noticed, was watching closely, with her hand ready to reach into her shoulder holster. Luke shook his head at her briskly.

"Is that a threat?" said Dodger, rolling his puny fists. Luckily Raziel placed his substantial bulk in between Dodger and the vampires.

"That is enough," the gargoyle rumbled, marble eyes shining.

The vampires relaxed a little, and Aurora let her arm hang loose.

"I apologise," said Evelyn. "The Artful Dodger is a little upset. It's been a hard few days."

The vampire nodded. "I understand. But I feel obliged to finish what I was saying. We've had a visitor at Clarence's. Several times in fact. A rather tenacious young lady called Amy Short who works for *The Times* newspaper. She is putting the pieces together, asking awkward questions."

"Perhaps this isn't the time to discuss things," said Raziel.

"Quite right," said the vampire, after a pause. "There will be other opportunities, not least at the council."

He stepped back, and Luke frowned, wondering what the vampire had meant by "the council". Some kind of vampire meeting?

"We wish you well, Evelyn Harker," said the vampire. As he walked away, he muttered something to the sewer troll, who nodded back.

The troll lumbered forward. "My condolences," said the creature, with a voice that sounded like water sucked down a plughole. Thankfully, considering the size and power of his grip, sewer trolls didn't shake hands. "Harker has always been a friend to the sewer trolls."

Drool spilled from his thick lips as he spoke, and Luke saw Evelyn trying not to gag at the stench of his breath.

"Thank you," she said.

"My name is Greb," said the troll. "I also wish to pay my respects and to thank the Immortals for your recent dealings with some renegade members of our kind."

Luke remembered the fight well, a few weeks back. A number of the trolls had broken their oath and begun to prey on humans – the homeless mostly, and also an underground civil engineer. It was a smelly escapade, but the Immortals had managed to capture the trolls responsible.

"It was our duty," Luke said.

"Yeah, no hard feelings," said Dodger.

The sewer troll remained where he was. Luke looked at the puddle of spit pooling at his feet and wondered if he could collect some of it for chemical analysis without anyone noticing.

"The vampire is right, I'm afraid," added Greb. "The Supernatural Council is concerned about your activities and the attention you are attracting."

Luke's ears pricked up. "I've never heard of the Supernatural Council."

Greb turned his watery eyes on Luke. He flipped his three-fingered hand over, and Luke saw he was wearing a golden ring, so tight the flesh of his middle finger bulged around it. The surface of the ring was engraved with a symbol, and Luke memorised it for later. A circle with a dot in the middle and four short lines at the compass points. It reminded him of a crosshair.

"This four-pointed circle represents the Council," said Greb. "We sewer trolls have been the Council's guardians for thousands of years. We protect the ancient site, and summon the members. But we have not called a Council for centuries. That is a mark of the severity of the situation. We will be discussing the best way to keep the existence of supernatural creatures hidden, and part of that will be a vote on the future of the Immortals."

"You can't do that," growled Aurora, speaking up for the first time as she strolled over.

The troll made a gesture a bit like a shrug, and a waft of something awful found its way into Luke's nostrils. He managed to twist the grimace into a half-smile.

"The Council is attended by representatives from many species. You could try to go against its decisions, but it would be . . . unwise."

Aurora looked about to speak again, but the troll held up a hand. "But please," he said. "I am not here as your enemy. You will have a say at the Council." The troll paused, and his translucent inner eyelids flickered as his eyes rolled upwards.

Luke flinched, staring at the troll. It was like the creature was having some sort of spasm. Evelyn's brow had furrowed in concern and Dodger was looking appalled. But then the troll's eyes returned to normal and he continued talking as if nothing had happened.

"I'm here to invite you officially to the Council, Miss Harker. You will represent the Immortals at the meeting."

Luke's confusion vanished, and his gaze snapped round to Evelyn.

"Me?" said Evelyn.

Luke almost said something too but managed to stop himself. *Why* not *Evelyn?* he supposed. But surely he should go as well. After all, it was Luke's father who had started the Immortals.

"I will discuss it with the others," Evelyn said. "The Immortals have no leader, and we take decisions together."

"Very well," said Greb. He reached into the pocket of his tunic, and took out a card. "Come to this address and I will explain everything you need to know about the Council, where it is being held and how to find the secret entrance, as well as the exact time to arrive. I must also give you your own ring, which will grant you passage past the guards."

Luke tried to see the address, but couldn't without making it too obvious. Evelyn's eyes scanned the card, before she passed it back.

"I've got it."

Luke wondered for a second if she'd purposely given it back, so Luke couldn't see it.

The sewer troll nodded its large head. "Once again, my condolences, Miss Harker."

Luke watched as Greb walked away, feeling a mixture of worry and defiance. Why would the Council vote to put an end to the Immortals? Could they really do it? Didn't they realise how close the world had come to destruction, if Sanakhte or Draka had succeeded?

"I need a drink," mumbled Dodger.

Luke wasn't sure what he needed, but he felt helpless. If the vote at the Council went against them, all his father's work, and everything Jonathan Harker had fought for, would come to an end.

CHAPTER 2

"Don't know about you two, but I was sort of hoping for a bust-up," said Dodger, slouching in the backseat of the car on the way to Clarence's, picking his teeth with a cocktail stick. "I mean, all those nutjobs in one place . . . " he paused, and looked at the vampire who was driving them, " . . . present company excepted, fella – but all those different ogres and cannibals and whatnot. Here, I've got a joke for you, Evelyn. Cheer you up a bit. A vampire, a werewolf and a witch walk into a bar—ouch!"

Luke had dug an elbow into him again, and this time he'd meant to do it hard. He wished Dodger had gone in the car with Aurora and Raziel, but that wouldn't have been sensible. Aurora Cage had a very short temper, especially in confined spaces, and he doubted

Dodger would have made it to the wake with all his limbs intact.

"It's all right," said Evelyn. She'd taken off her hat and veil. Her eyes were red-rimmed and puffy. "Dodger's right. I do need to cheer up. Dad wouldn't want to see me like this."

"Glad to hear it, luv," said Dodger. "The party'll sort out your spirits. Nothing like a good knees-up to say farewell to the dear departed." He raised an imaginary glass in a toast.

"Did either of you see the man in the mask?" Luke asked.

"The tall chap?" said Dodger. "Yeah, I did wonder about him. You think he gate-crashed?"

"My father had a long life and many acquaintances," said Evelyn. "I'm sure there's nothing sinister in it."

"I think he was watching *me*," said Luke.

"You would," said Dodger, laughing. "You're a raving egotist."

They arrived at Clarence's in West London just before 6.30am. Luke had sent an open invite to the vampire gentlemen's club, and it had been the committee there who offered to host the wake, as befitted a member of Harker's standing. It was still a thrill as they pulled up outside though. And maybe a little scary. After all, the last time they'd been here, disguised as vampires themselves, Dodger had blagged their way in. It hadn't ended well.

Luke exited onto the pavement. The street was already fairly busy with people going to work, and delivery vans. Goodness knows what they'd make of those coming to the wake, but Luke had arranged for some of the stranger guests, such as the sewer trolls, the Ghouls and Raziel, to enter via the underground garage.

Dodger came next, springing out, straightening his coat-tails and offering Evelyn a hand. Aurora's car pulled up behind, and Luke went to her door. He was about to open it, when he noticed she was loading rounds into the chamber of the gun on her lap.

"Expecting trouble?" he asked through the open window.

She tipped back her head. "Do *you* think this is safe?"

"Water under the bridge," said Dodger, with a dismissive wave.

"They invited us," added Luke, shrugging. He hardly remembered the last visit because he'd been out of it and badly injured. He was actually looking forward to a proper snoop around. Vampires were so secretive, but they probably kept good records. And because they didn't age, he hoped to bump into a *really* old one with some good stories.

There were five or six major vampire lines that Luke knew of, and since the 1950s, there were quite strict rules about turning new humans – on the occasions they did go "hunting", they were supposed to bite to kill. Animal blood lacked the particular protein that vampires needed for nourishment, so many opted instead for sustenance from blood banks – it was as close to a vegetarian option as vampires came, and a victimless way to quench one's thirst.

Aurora clambered out, and the car pulled away. As it did, Luke's peripheral vision caught a metallic glimmer to his left. He spun around and spotted the masked man watching from beside a lamp post across the street, with a hood pulled up over his head. He alone was stationary among the flow of pedestrians. Dodger, Aurora and Evelyn were already heading up the red-carpeted steps under the Clarence's awning.

The stranger held his gaze and Luke couldn't escape the challenge in the stare. It was more than curiosity. And then with a jolt Luke remembered where he had seen that mask before. His father had had one similar in his study – Etruscan, if he remembered correctly. Victor's housekeeper had caught him trying it on once, but promised to keep it a secret. Was this the same artefact? Surely not . . .

As Luke took a step off the kerb towards him, the masked man turned abruptly and began to march away.

"Hey, wait!" Luke called.

A few people turned, Evelyn included, but he wasn't sure if they'd seen the man, because he'd slipped down an alley. Luke darted across the street, causing a black cab to swerve.

"Luke, come back!" shouted Evelyn.

He skidded around the corner into the alley – a rubbish-strewn passage between tall, windowless buildings on either side. The masked figure began to run.

You're not getting away that easily, thought Luke.

Luke could achieve the speed of a hundred-metre runner, and he took off in pursuit, the ground flying beneath him. The masked stranger vanished round another bend and Luke was there two seconds later. His prey was quick too though, taking long pounding strides. But there was a dead-end ahead – an office building three storeys high. *Got you!*

As they both hurtled towards it, Luke wondered if he could even bring the man down. He had his lightning blade, but he didn't want to hurt the stranger; just talk to him. The man looked to be unarmed. He seemed more afraid than anything.

"Stop!" he yelled.

At the base of the wall, the man dropped into a crouch and pushed off the ground. Luke jerked his chin in astonishment as the jump lifted him off the ground. The man reached up, and his fingertips caught on a piece of guttering twenty feet above the alleyway. *That's some jump.*

The gutter began to crack and come away at once. Luke caught his breath. *He's going to fall.* But somehow, with a deep grunt, the masked stranger swung further up, and fastened onc hand over the roof's lip. He pulled himself up with ease and disappeared over the edge without looking back.

Luke reached for his satchel at his back, to extract the grapple gun attachment he kept inside it. The bag wasn't there, and he remembered he'd agreed not to wear it for the funeral. *That's the last time I leave it behind.* Luke jumped halfway up the building, fingertips clasping hold of a narrow window ledge. He pulled his toes up onto the lip, hugging his body to the glass window as he stood up.

Inside, a man was sipping from a steaming mug in a small office kitchen. He saw Luke, and dropped it on the floor, leaping back as hot tea splashed his trousers. Luke looked up, and sprang another storey.

This window had the blinds drawn. He looked down, and swallowed thickly. Fall here, and just about every bone would shatter. He took a deep breath, and jumped again. This time he reached the top, and hauled himself onto a pitched roof.

Luke rolled and stood up, panting. He couldn't see the man anywhere.

A burst of pigeons behind a chimney stack to the south. Luke sprinted in that direction and saw the masked figure coming out from behind a chimney, roof slates scattering from his feet. *So much for us keeping a low profile.*

Luke was gaining. The masked man ran clumsily now. *He's getting tired.* They leapt across onto a modern flat roof, chasing between air-vents and antennae. At the far side, the man climbed onto the parapet, arms wheeling a moment for balance. Luke slowed as he approached. The street below was too wide to jump across and reach the buildings on the far side.

"Stop there," he said. "There's nowhere else to go. I just want to talk."

The masked man turned, breathing hard, looking over his shoulder at Luke. Now he was closer, Luke wasn't so sure he'd read the eyes well before. They seemed desperate, even fearful.

"Who are you?" Luke asked.

With a small hop, the man stepped off the edge of the building and plummeted.

Luke's heart leapt into his stomach. It was too far . . . He heard a scream.

With a sick feeling in his gut, he rushed to the edge and looked down. Four storeys below, the masked figure was on his hands and knees, already standing up. People on the pavement were pointing, dumbstruck, others running over.

"That's impossible," Luke breathed.

The masked figure was clearly hurt. He dragged one leg as he stumbled towards the road. He had to rest a hand on the bonnet of a car.

He hadn't seen the bus hurtling down the street.

"No!" Luke yelled. As the masked figure stepped between the cars into the road, the bus's brakes screeched. Too late. It must have been doing close to thirty miles an hour as the thudding impact lifted the stranger off his feet. His body turned limply in the air, landing a few metres further down the road before sliding and fetching up against the kerb. He lay still, and the bus came to a hissing halt.

Bystanders began to crowd closely. One looked up at the building's precipice. Luke ducked out of sight, unsure what to do. He couldn't leave the man there. And not just because of what the vampire had said at the funeral about keeping out of the news. Luke felt responsible. The man had jumped because of *him*.

He ran to the side of the building, and peered into a quieter road. He picked his way down as fast as he could, then rounded the corner. The bus driver had stepped out now, holding his head in his hands as he walked towards the victim in a daze. "I didn't see him. He just jumped out . . . "

There were so many people already. A man in a suit was calling an ambulance, his face pale.

Luke pushed past them all.

"Let me through!"

His feet became heavy as he reached the body, then he stumbled as the truth hit home. The stranger was dead.

"Why's he wearing a mask?" someone said.

No one had touched the man yet, he saw. They looked bewildered and afraid.

"Is anyone here a doctor?" said another.

Luke crouched beside the fallen stranger, feeling for his pulse with a sinking heart. *Why? Why did he jump?* No pulse. He was dead and it was Luke's fault. *If I hadn't frightened him, chased him . . .* The bus must have finished what the fall had started. He felt suddenly protective. *All these people, gawping . . .*

He gripped the man's arm.

"What are you doing, kid?"

With the arm looped over his shoulder, Luke hoisted the masked man to his feet with a grunt of exertion. He must have weighed close to twenty stone, and it tested Luke's enhanced strength to its limits. "Look, he's fine!" he said. "Just needs to walk it off."

"You shouldn't move him," said a woman. "He might have spinal injuries."

But Luke was already staggering away. To his relief, no one followed. Around the corner, he waved to a black cab. It slowed, then the driver squinted at Luke's companion and accelerated away. Two more did the same, and Luke was beginning to feel desperate. *The police won't be long, surely.* The fourth taxi did stop, and the driver wound down his window.

"Had a few, has he?" he asked.

Luke nodded quickly. "Yeah, he's my uncle."

"Not gonna be sick in my cab, is he? It'll be a fifty quid fine if he does, but I'd sooner have a clean cab than your money."

"He'll be fine, I promise," said Luke. "Can you take us to Southwark Cathedral please?"

"Hop in, guv," said the cabbie. "Though I think he's beyond the Good Lord's help. Fry up's the thing he needs."

Luke clambered in, and managed to manhandle his companion into the seat beside him. The skin of the stranger's huge hands was rough, the knuckles scarred as if from fighting. In the rear-view mirror, the taxi-driver seemed to notice the mask for the first time.

"Must have been some party," he said.

"It was," Luke replied.

"Put his seat-belt on, will you?" said the driver.

Luke did as he was told, not that it was going to do much for the masked giant now.

Back at Southwark Cathedral, he paid the driver and carried the dead man to the concealed elevator in the churchyard. Panting from the effort, he heaved the masked man inside, then hit the button for the medical labs in the crypt. As the elevator descended, Luke's mind was whirring. He kept replaying the image of the masked man stepping over the edge of the building, over and over. Then the bus as it ploughed into him.

Luke felt a cringe of dread, thinking of the camera phones that could have been filming the chase. With the Supernatural Council meeting coming up, Luke could have caused the Immortals' reputation real damage. He thought about calling Evelyn, and letting her know what had happened, but something, maybe guilt, held him back – he knew they'd be angry at him for being so reckless, and missing the wake. Besides, she had enough to worry about.

After the elevator doors opened, Luke hauled the huge limp corpse through the stone-flagged crypt, lined with sarcophagi and glowing from the flat screens hanging on the grey walls. He opened the reinforced door to the medical room. As the lights inside blinked on, they reflected off the metal tables gleaming with instruments.

Luke managed to haul the corpse onto the examination bed – the very same one where Evelyn and her father had woken Luke from his 160-year slumber, confused and with a body no longer quite his own. He'd thought at the time that it might be some kind of afterlife, and in many ways the truth – that he had been brought back from the dead – was even harder to believe.

Luke wiped the sweat from his forehead with the back of his sleeve. He switched on the ceiling lamps to inspect the body in front of him. Seven feet now seemed an over-estimate. The body was two metres in height at most. Tall, but not drastically unusual. The man was broad, with massive, powerful shoulders, but the rest of him was almost gaunt, as if he hadn't eaten much for a long time.

He inspected the mask. As he'd thought, it was no

costume-shop disguise, but finely wrought metal. It was certainly at least Roman, if not older. *But did it really belong to my father?* The back of it, where it extended below the man's chin, over his ears and scalp, actually looked more recent and seemed to be made of a different metal, perhaps a coloured alloy. It was perfectly designed to fit this individual's features. Luke tucked the hood further away from the head, and peered closer. There was some sort of clasp behind the ears – an interlocking mechanism. Gingerly, he fitted his fingertips under the edge and released it. The mask lifted, becoming looser. Luke hesitated for a moment, then prised it off the man's face.

When he saw what lay beneath, he struggled not to look away.

He'd seen many horrific things in his new life. Sanakhte's mummified corpse rising from the dead, bodies consumed by evil spirits, all manner of gory deaths, but the face beneath the mask was somehow worse because it filled him with pity as well as fear. The man had clearly been badly burned. His nose was mostly gone, as well as his top lip, giving him a grimace of exposed teeth. He had only one ear. His eye-sockets were uneven, the skin around them and the closed eyelids melted. The whole of the stranger's face was covered in mottled scar tissue and his head was bald of all but a few wisps of hair.

Luke swallowed, wondering what it could have been like to suffer such awful injuries.

Who are you?

The man obviously had superhuman capabilities, but he had no fangs, and a quick look at his hands and nails showed no sign of lycanthropic hybridity. Not a vampire or werewolf then. Despite the deformities, his physiology appeared human.

To Luke's surprise, he saw that though the man's tunic was torn a little in places from the bus collision, there were no signs of any blood or flesh wounds. Trying to put his distaste aside, he reached for the buttons at the top of the man's tunic, wondering if the scarring was confined to the head, or if the entire body would be the same.

Under his collar, the deceased man was wearing a simple silver chain around his neck, and from it hung a shining pendant. It looked too delicate for such a brutish figure, and Luke held it in his palm to inspect it more closely. A ring of flowers, delicately engraved, surrounded two sets of intertwining initials.

VF and *EF*.

Luke drew a sharp breath and the temperature in the

room dipped. Or perhaps it was just his blood pumping cold around his body. It couldn't be a coincidence, could it?

Victor and Elizabeth Frankenstein.

His mother and father.

Luke blinked, in case his eyes were deceiving him. He felt suddenly vindicated. Angry, even. His suspicion about the mask had proved correct. It *had* belonged to his father.

But his parents had been dead for decades. His mother had perished in a fever following childbirth, his father not long after the first battle with Sanakhte, working himself to death in an effort to bring Luke back from the dead. Yet this man had their names inscribed on a keepsake. How could he even have known them, unless he was alive back in Victorian times? Was he their friend?

Luke's mind fixed upon a darker explanation. This pendant – it wasn't something a man would wear. It was a piece of women's jewellery, a love token, and surely there was only one person it could have belonged to. Luke's mother.

Had this scarred man stolen the pendant from her, and the mask from his father?

Luke jolted as he saw the burned features twitch a

fraction. But the body lay still again and the seconds passed. Luke's heart slowed once more. It was unsettling, but everyone involved with dead bodies knew they sometimes underwent post-mortem spasms. He returned to the buttons on the man's jacket, following the scar tissue across his chest.

An arm shot up and gripped Luke's wrist with astonishing force.

Luke tried to pull away but couldn't.

Then the stranger's eyes opened.

CHAPTER 3

Evelyn sank onto the banquette, listening to the antique harpsichord tinkling from the corner of the stone-flagged chamber of Clarence's main drawing room. Thick velvet curtains hung across the door and the furniture was a mixture of luxury items from across the ages, brought in to cater to the tastes of their varied clientele. Wing-back armchairs, art deco tables inlaid with glass mosaic, and dark mahogany bureaus. Likewise the pictures on the walls came from different centuries. If they had anything in common, it was their sombre mood. Most depicted macabre or depressing scenes of corpse-strewn battlefields or shipwrecks, or simply dark modern pieces suggesting grief or mental turmoil, all to fit the temperament of the vampiric members.

Evelyn pictured the scene the last time the Immortals

had been here, fighting for their lives against Sanakhte's lieutenant, Minnakht – an eight-foot jackal-headed demon armed with two curved scimitars – as well as hordes of undead archaeologists cursed to serve the dark pharaoh for eternity. Several vampires had been staked through the heart, Luke had almost been killed, most of the furniture had been smashed to pieces, and there were bloodstains on the walls and ceiling.

It could have gone better.

Thankfully, since the Immortals defeated Sanakhte, apologies had been made and accepted, and all was forgiven. The management had spruced the place up nicely in the intervening months.

Evelyn surveyed the vampires around the room, dressed in various clothes from different periods, including a couple of women in eighties power suits with frankly odd-looking shoulder pads. An austere looking man with a grey ponytail wore a doublet, perhaps from the Civil War period in the mid-seventeenth century. Or perhaps he just liked those fashions. Many were sipping goblets of blood, all fetched up from Clarence's renowned cellars. Rumour had it you could buy a bottle of red from the Napoleonic Wars if you had the money.

It all tasted the same to Evelyn. Not that she was thirsty anyway.

"Where *is* he?" she asked Raziel.

The gargoyle shrugged. "Master Luke will come soon, I am sure," he said.

Evelyn frowned. "I really can't see why he ran off like that. I mean, today of all days."

Raziel, as so often, said nothing. His faintly glowing white eyes were scanning the room, ever vigilant. Much to Dodger's ongoing disappointment, there still hadn't been a "bust-up". All the other supernatural creatures were on best behaviour. The werewolves were keeping to themselves near the bookshelves, though Evelyn noticed that several volumes of "The Werewolf Vampire War of 1798" were on prominent display (the vampires had won that one). Aurora Cage stood with a few of the *Canes Umbrarum*, doing her best to look interested in the conversation, though she often said she couldn't stand more than five minutes in the company of the prim, aristocratic werewolf society members. Or "snobs who liked to groom themselves too much" as Aurora put it.

The ghoul from the funeral was drifting around, generally making people feel uncomfortable with his intense, unblinking stare, and Professor Tadic and a few other sorcerers were remarking about a TV magician who'd accidentally cut his assistant in half. They seemed to find it hilarious based on the guffaws that peppered their conversation. Another sorcerer was making the suit of armour in the corner move – until one of the club's waiters asked her to stop. Some sewer trolls and river sprites were in the middle of a heated conversation about litter in the Thames.

Luke would be really enjoying this, thought Evelyn. She imagined him frantically scribbling in that scrapbook of his.

Could it be that he was just being childish, avoiding her because of the whole Council invite thing? She'd seen the look on his face when Greb gave the card to her – disappointed and hurt. It was true his father had been the founder of the Immortals, but since his death it was *her* dad who'd run things. Anyway, they didn't really have a leader as such. Each member in the group had their own talents. No one bossed anyone else around, and like she'd told the sewer troll, decisions were taken as a team.

He's got no reason to be jealous. And he should *be here.*

"Excuse me, Miss Harker?"

A young man was approaching, very slim, with blonde hair, wearing a double-breasted black suit. From his pallid features she realised he must be a vampire, though she hadn't seen him at the funeral earlier. "My name is Baines," he said. "I'm a solicitor, working on behalf of your father. Would you care to follow me to a more private room so we can discuss certain matters?"

Evelyn stood up, intrigued. "Of course." She hadn't known her father even had a solicitor.

Mr Baines began to walk towards one of the curtains that covered a stone-arched doorway. He pushed it aside with a slender hand, to allow Evelyn to pass. As Raziel stooped under as well, the lawyer cocked his head. "I'm afraid this is a private matter, Mr ... ?"

Raziel treated him to a stony stare, then shouldered past.

"Don't worry," said Evelyn. "He's a trusted friend."

Baines straightened his tie and flashed a smile. "Very well."

They went down a corridor a short way, past a dining room, then Baines took out a key and opened an iron-studded door. Inside was an office with a huge, leather-covered desk, more bookshelves, and comfortable chairs.

"Take a seat, please," said the solicitor.

Evelyn did so, but Raziel assumed a standing position with his back to the door.

Sitting behind the desk, Baines placed both hands on the desk's top.

"Forgive the intrusion at such a sensitive time," he

began, "but your father's instructions on the matter were quite clear."

"Did you know him well?" asked Evelyn.

"Very," said Baines with a nod. "He was a great man and will never be forgotten." He opened a drawer to his right and took out a leather document case, spreading it in front of him. "First, a few straightforward matters. According to Jonathan Harker's last will and testament, all of his worldly possessions are to pass to you, Miss Harker. There are several bank accounts, some property, and rather a lot in storage." He passed a sheaf of papers across the table. "These contain a summary, and there is a contact at the top of the first page in case you'd like to discuss anything."

Evelyn's eyes flicked over the paper. She knew about most of it – the château in Reims, France, the Scottish loch-side folly – but she'd had no idea he actually owned property in Transylvania.

Mr Baines slid a simple key towards her. "This opens a vault in the Bank of England," he said. "As I understand it, your father had substantial jewellery and cash deposits."

"Thank you," Evelyn said, pocketing the key. This all felt so formal, like a business transaction, and it made her miss her father all the more. "You suggested there might be something not so *straightforward*," she said.

The solicitor nodded. "And finally, there is this." He reached into his inner breast pocket, and handed across a simple cream envelope. On the front, in her father's writing, it said simply: "Evelyn."

The envelope was patterned and embossed. She wondered if the stationery was Victorian. It smelled old, and the edges were slightly brown.

"Shall I open it now?" she asked.

"As you wish," said Mr Baines. He stood up. "I will leave you in private."

Raziel stood aside to let him leave and Evelyn reached for a dagger-shaped letter-opener beside the desk-lamp. She sliced it open.

Inside was a single folded sheaf of heavy paper. She spread it in front of her and read.

My darling Evelyn,

If you are reading this, then I am gone. Do not grieve for me too much. I have lived a longer life than I ever could have imagined. Longer than any person's due.

My dear daughter, you have been a constant source of joy – and I doubt there has ever been a prouder father. So many happy memories, but as I write now one stands out most clearly. Our holidays on Iona, with your mother and little Quincey too. Searching for crabs on that rocky bay on the eastern shore. I wonder if you remember it, darling?

Evelyn paused. In truth, the memory was a dim one – she must have been eight or nine at the time – and it merged and mingled with others from when her younger brother was still alive.

The one great regret I have in passing is that I will be leaving you behind, though I know you do not need your papa any more, and haven't for some time.

Evelyn saw a tear hit the paper and wiped her eyes. With every word, she heard her father's gentle voice.

Your resourcefulness, intelligence, and kindness will stand you in great stead, and of course you have another family who will always be there at your side – the Immortals. Time and circumstance will test those friendships, but you must never let them go.

"Are you all right?" asked Raziel. He rested a stone hand on her shoulder.

Evelyn nodded. She'd almost reached the end of the letter.

There is one last thing I must pass on to you. At the Bank of England you will find a cache of papers belonging to my dear friend Victor Frankenstein. They contain a secret that I have guarded for a long time. Now it is up to you. You must not tell anyone that the papers exist – at least not until you have read what they contain. I am sorry to pass this burden on to you but I have no choice. It is a duty I must fulfil.

Live your life, my daughter, and do your duties by the Immortals. But don't forget to have some fun too!

Your loving father,

Jonathan.

Evelyn folded the paper again, and sat back in the chair. She felt the tears still on her cheeks, but she was intrigued. Secret papers? Why on earth were they being left to her, if they belonged to Victor? Surely Luke should be the recipient of his father's possessions. Yet that expressly was not her father's instruction. She was to keep the secret to herself. And why was it so important that she received this letter today? So many questions . . .

She wanted to go meet Greb the sewer troll later but there would be time to visit the Bank of England before that.

Then she would have some answers.

CHAPTER 4

Luke tried to yank his hand away, but the man held on with an iron grip. A series of emotions – fear, confusion, anger – wrestled in the stranger's scarred features.

"Get off me!" shouted Luke.

The man sat up, looking around in jerking movements, taking in the room. Luke summoned his lightning blade, but the man had his wrist so tight it wouldn't slide from its housing beneath his skin. Instead, Luke grabbed the angled ceiling lamp over the exam table and pulled it down onto the man's head. Sparks fizzled and glass scattered over the table and floor, leaving only the dull glow of the lanterns from the crypt through the open door. The giant let go, grunting.

Luke backed off, and now the searing hot electric

blade shot out from his wrist, humming faintly. "Don't come any closer!" he said.

But the man swung his long legs off the bed and strode purposefully towards him. Then he stopped, eyes looking at something over Luke's shoulder. With a howl, he threw his arms over his head. Luke turned and saw nothing but the reflection in the sterile, stainless steel medical cabinets hanging on the wall.

The hulking figure scrambled away, cowering, into a corner of the room, cradling his head as if utterly terrified.

Luke let his weapon retract into his arm but kept his distance.

"Are you okay?" he asked.

"My mask!" the man said. "My mask!"

Luke saw the metal mask on the floor by the leg of the table. "It's here," he said, scooping it up.

"Please! Give it to me!" pleaded the man. His voice was deep, the accent maybe eastern European.

Luke wondered if this was some sort of trick, but he approached nonetheless, extending his arm, ready to spring back if the stranger tried anything. A huge hand whipped out and snatched the mask from him. The man replaced it, clicking the covering into place. His chest was heaving, glistening with sweat as if he'd run a sprint. *Some sort of panic attack . . .* thought Luke. *He couldn't fake that.*

"Sorry for hitting you with the lamp," said Luke. The man didn't reply, staring round at the base in confusion. "I brought you here," said Luke. "You were in a traffic accident."

The eyes behind the mask stared at him.

"Who are you?" Luke asked.

Slowly the stranger's breathing calmed, and Luke gave him time.

"My name is Adam," said the man at last. He spoke with an odd formality, and along with the accent, Luke guessed English wasn't his first language.

"I'm Luke."

"I know this," said the man. "I have been watching you."

The words were uttered impassively, with no hint of emotion.

"I saw," said Luke, smiling to put the stranger at ease. "You're not a very good spy."

If the man smiled back, Luke couldn't tell. "I wanted . . . to talk to you. But I did not know how."

Luke frowned. "Well, you almost got yourself killed by a number 168 bus."

The man let out a rasp of laughter, though it contained

little joy. "I cannot be killed by a bus," he said. "I'm not sure I can be killed by anything. Your father made sure of that."

Luke bristled. "You knew my father?"

Adam nodded. "Of course. He . . . he was my father too."

For a moment the room seemed to sway. "What?"

"Victor Frankenstein created me," said Adam. Then, with a hint of pride. "I was his *first* son."

Luke put a hand on the bed behind him to steady himself. Could that be true? He thought of John, Victor's creation who had always been there as he grew up – harvested limbs sewn together and brought back to life. He had been like an older brother to Luke – an older brother who never aged. Three times as strong as a normal man, but kind, loyal and trusting.

Luke had never even suspected that John was not the first, but now he thought about it, it made sense. His father was a scientist, an experimenter. Was it not highly likely there had been experiments that . . . failed? The evidence pointed that way. "The pendant," he muttered. "And the mask."

Adam's hand touched the delicate piece of jewellery around his neck. "I took this, from our mother," he said.

"You stole it?" said Luke.

Adam bowed his head. "I wanted something to remember them by. When I left Austria." The words were full of sadness.

Luke offered him his hand. The giant looked at it for a moment, then reached out. As he did, Luke saw the scars of rough stitching below his wrist. Perhaps the hand and arm had come from different cadavers. John had been scarred too, but the marks had been neater, more faded. Victor Frankenstein's techniques had obviously improved with time. Luke hoisted the man to his feet.

"Why did you leave my father?" asked Luke. "Did you run away?"

Adam's head twitched and his body stiffened. He looked towards the ceiling. "Someone is here," he said.

Luke heard the voices now as well. Dodger's patter. "I tell you, I'm stuffed to the gills. Those vamps make some fang-tastic canapés. Get it? *Fang*-tastic."

"Hilarious," said Aurora Cage.

"Don't worry. They are my friends," said Luke to Adam.

The masked man stayed put as Luke went to the stairs leading to the main chamber.

"I didn't think much to those chicken things though," said Dodger. "But I guess blood-suckers have an aversion to steak." He paused. "Come on, you get it – *stake*! As in the wooden variety. You're a tough crowd, y'know."

Aurora groaned.

"Enough," said Evelyn. "We need to focus. Greb said the Supernatural Council meeting isn't far off."

Luke came through the door and they all jumped. Apart from Aurora, who drew her Smith and Wesson and pointed it at Luke in a fraction of a second. He shot up his arms. "Only me!" he said.

Aurora rolled her eyes, spun the gun and holstered it again. "I don't like surprises," she said.

"Where did you get to?" said Evelyn with a scowl.

"Sorry," said Luke. He explained about the masked figure at the funeral, the chase and the collision with the bus. And, finally, the remarkable identity of the stranger. "He was my dad's first creation, before John. He's called Adam."

Evelyn's eyebrows raised in shock. "I never heard Victor or Dad mentioning anything about another creature."

"You sure he's telling the truth?" Aurora growled. "It doesn't smell right to me."

"I'm sure," said Luke. Leaning back, he called out, "Adam, come up here."

The other Immortals watched him closely as heavy

footsteps sounded on the metal stairs, then Adam appeared, looming over Luke. Aurora's hand dropped to her pistol once more.

"Er ... hi!" said Dodger after a moment's silence. "Nice mask."

"Does he talk?" asked Aurora, watching Adam warily, fingers hovering over her holster.

"I do," said Adam.

"You shouldn't have brought him here, Luke," Evelyn snapped, turning to Luke.

Luke was startled. "What choice did I have?" he replied.

Evelyn tapped her chin. "Hmmm, well maybe instead of charging after a random stranger in the first place, you could have come to my dad's wake."

"He's not a random stranger," replied Luke.

"Evelyn's right, kid," growled Aurora. "We don't know anything about him."

"What you been up to all these years, eh?" said Dodger, eyes narrowing. "Why come back now? Seems fishy if you ask me."

Adam looked at Luke, searching for help. But before Luke could defend him, Evelyn spoke in a contrite but formal tone. "Thank you for coming to my father's funeral, Adam. I'm sure Dad would have been intrigued to meet you. We are all interested in finding out what you've been up to for the past two hundred years – though we have some pressing matters to attend to right now. Please understand, you have to leave, and you must not come back here. It is crucial our base remains secret." She held out a hand, but Adam just shrank away.

Luke was panicking. Adam was clearly unpredictable, his emotional state like a young child's. If he left now, who knew if he'd ever come back. "I want to talk to him," said Luke.

Evelyn's face was hard. "He has to leave. Now. In case you forgot, we have a Supernatural Council meeting we need to prepare for."

Luke felt anger grow inside him. "Who made you the boss?" As soon as the words left his mouth, he regretted them.

"We have no *leader*," said Evelyn, sharply. "Or maybe you think *you* should be in charge?"

Luke felt a hand on his arm. "I will go," said Adam.

Evelyn nodded. "Good. We'll show you to the surface." She began to walk towards the elevators, with Adam trailing after her. Luke followed, but on the way he scooped something from the lab table. He couldn't risk this link with the past – with his father – slipping from his grasp. The others wouldn't like it, but he didn't have a choice. He climbed into the elevator with Evelyn and Adam.

"Goodbye, brother," Adam said to Luke softly, as the elevator climbed smoothly to ground level. The doors opened, and Adam walked out of the Tomb of the Angel, into the graveyard beyond.

Luke stepped after him. "Come back in a few days," he said. "Wait by the front gates of the churchyard," he added, after a frown from Evelyn. "We'll see you on the cameras." Adam said nothing. Luke touched the giant's elbow as he shook his hand. At the same time he fixed the tracker. It was hardly bigger than a pinhead, almost invisible against the dark fabric of Adam's sleeve. Then he turned and re-joined Evelyn in the lift.

Luke watched Adam's broad back as he shuffled away, treading heavily among the gravestones. Evelyn paused with her finger over the elevator button, as if about to say something. But she thought better of it, and they descended in silence.

As soon as they'd reached the main chamber, Evelyn took on a business-like composure. Raziel and Aurora were analysing screens in one corner, while Dodger lay on a couch with his hat tipped forward over his eyes. He pushed it up as Evelyn began to speak.

"Right, we need to start building evidence for our

case. The Council can't shut us down. Let's make a list of who's likely to be there, anticipate their arguments ..."

Luke hung back. Normally, nothing could have stopped him being involved in planning the case that could decide the Immortals' future. But his anger with Evelyn hadn't completely gone away, and the meeting with Adam had unsettled him, leaving questions whirling around his brain. Why had his father kept Adam's existence secret? Why did he leave? What made him track Luke down now? "I'll be there in a bit," he said, walking past them all.

"Come on, fella," said Dodger. "No need to sulk."

"I just need some time to think," said Luke. He took the stairs to the living quarters, leaving the others to their discussion.

Over the past few weeks, Luke had gradually adapted his bedroom to suit his tastes. Apart from the bed and wardrobe and desk, all sourced from a vintage Victorian furniture store, there were posters tacked to the walls – mostly for martial arts movies, and bands he liked. The base's interactive computer, BIOS – or Bayesian Interpretative Operating System – could automatically upload the Top 40 albums from the last sixty years directly into his cerebellum to save time, just as it had given him black belt proficiency in ju jitsu and jeet kune do – the martial arts star Bruce Lee's fighting style. But there were some things Luke didn't mind doing the old-fashioned way. He was slowly working his way through the 1980s at the moment, and put on some punk rock, which fitted his mood perfectly. He went to the heavy bag hanging from the ceiling, and gave it a few half-hearted punches.

What's wrong with them all?

Couldn't any of them have put themselves in his shoes? Surely they could understand why Luke wanted to find out who Adam was – why he had brought him back to the base.

It was Evelyn he was most disappointed in. If it hadn't been the day of Jonathan Harker's funeral, perhaps the others wouldn't have sided with her so readily. Sure, she talked about the Immortals being a democracy, but did she really mean it? He guessed it was only natural for her to see herself as the leader – she had been a member a lot longer than Luke, and had more experience. And it wasn't too hard to see where the Immortals were coming from in their distrust. Luke wondered if *he* would trust Adam if he was in their position? Maybe not.

But I wouldn't just have thrown him out like that.

He thumped the bag harder, enjoying the reverberation up his arm. He threw in a few kicks and elbows as well, gradually building up speed.

The others would be annoyed about the tracker,

if they found out – Luke should be focusing on the Supernatural Council meeting. No reason they should find out though. Anyway, they couldn't expect him just to watch Adam drift off into the sunset.

Luke stopped working the bag, went to the sink in the corner of the room, splashing water on his face. As he was doing so, his eyes fell on his bookshelf. Among the modern editions of Dickens were several much older, leather-bound volumes. Victor Frankenstein's journals.

So far Luke had avoided reading too much of them – hearing his father's voice through the words he had written was painful. But where better to find out about Adam? And, if he showed the others the evidence in Victor's own hand, they'd be more inclined to believe Adam's story and look upon him more kindly.

Luke dried his hands, and pulled several volumes from the shelves, laying them on his bed. Though they contained the records of a man of such meticulous scientific method, the journals themselves were a chaotic mess. As soon as Victor had reached the end of one, he'd started another, even if he was mid-entry. Writing that began in neat rows often spiralled out of control, filling the margins. Blotting and crossings out were common.

Luke found the ones relating to John's "birth", in 1848. Skipping back, the entries became more sporadic, and shorter. They dried up completely around Luke's birth, the same year. Luke guessed why – the death of Elizabeth, his mother, just after giving birth to Luke, must have hit his father hard. Moving further back still, Luke got a shock. There were several pages ripped from the journal entirely, leaving only the jagged edges of the torn paper.

Luke had no proof, but he suspected the missing pages had dealt with Adam. Had his father been ashamed of him? Determined that no record of the experiments ever reached the light of day. He imagined Victor Frankenstein feeding the torn evidence to the fire in his study.

There were still so many questions to answer, and only one person who could.

"BIOS, locate tracker 1 please," said Luke.

The screen on the wall blinked to life, and zoned in on an aerial map of London. A red dot was moving slowly alongside the River Thames, heading eastwards.

Luke approached the screen, reaching out to touch it, following it with a fingertip.

"Where are you going?" he whispered.

A pounding knock on the door startled him, and Luke turned off the screen manually.

"What is it?" he said.

Dodger entered, eyes wide and alert. "Look sharp, mate!" he said. "We've got trouble."

CHAPTER 5

Back in the main room of the base, the other Immortals were gathered around a bank of monitors. As Luke paced over, he saw the screens were showing CCTV footage from various hidden cameras above ground in the Southwark Cathedral churchyard. A woman was walking around the Tomb of the Angel, inspecting it.

"Any ideas who she is?" said Dodger, as he and Luke stopped by the others.

The woman entered the tomb, and Luke held his breath. The door to the elevator was well disguised, and the buttons were fingerprint sensitive so there would be no way she could get down into the base itself. But it was still worrying. Her face drifted close to the camera. Brown hair, cut short. Wide-spaced eyes, which were frowning. She wore an off-white coat loosely belted around the waist, and carried a leather handbag.

"She doesn't look like a werewolf or a vampire," said Evelyn.

Then Luke spotted something hanging around her neck – some sort of card on a chain.

"BIOS, zoom on her neck," said Luke.

The footage enlarged, but only the corner of the card showed.

"Hello?" said the woman, and they all jumped.

"Who's she talking to?" asked Dodger.

"Us," said Aurora. "She knows there's a camera. Listen, I don't much like this. Shall I . . . deal with her?"

"What do you mean?" asked Evelyn.

Aurora looked at her and shrugged. "What do you *want* me to mean?"

Dodger opened his coat to reveal a number of vials. He gestured to one. "If we're getting rid of her, may I suggest arsenic? Poison of choice when I grew up. Pretty quick, if you know how to dose."

"We're not going to kill her!" said Luke. "We don't even know who she is. BIOS, wind back footage real-time on camera 4."

The images on one of the screens began to rewind, the clock counting in reverse. The camera itself was mounted in the stone angel's eye-socket, concealed by a fake streak of bird excrement. The woman walked backwards from the tomb towards the small iron gate at the edge of the churchyard which was kept locked. She hopped over in reverse and disappeared around a corner.

"Play, slow-mo," said Luke.

The footage inched forward. They saw the woman arrive at the railings, looking left and right, then place her hands on the railings, and vault over.

"Pause and zoom."

As BIOS enlarged, Luke touched the screen to bring the right area into focus. The card had spilled out from beneath the V of the coat. The screen resolved from pixels to a smooth image as BIOS zoomed again.

The card read: "PRESS. Amy Short, Reporter. *The Times.*"

"Oh, great!" said Evelyn. "A journalist."

"Perhaps it is the same one the vampire spoke of," said Raziel.

"Might have something to do with this," said Dodger. He spun round his mobile phone and Luke read the headline. *"Boy flees bus collision carrying corpse: police seek witnesses."*

Evelyn grabbed the phone, scrolled down, and rolled her eyes. "Oh, this just gets better all the time." She showed Luke a picture of himself, holding up Adam. Only the side of his face was showing.

"It's not all that clear," he muttered.

"Don't worry, there's a video too," said Evelyn. "Luke, you've really messed up. She's followed you here, somehow."

Luke didn't see how that was possible. He'd been careful, hadn't he? He was always on the lookout when returning to the base.

"I know you're in there!" said Amy Short straight into Camera 1. "I just want to talk to you."

"Maybe we should let her in," said Luke.

The others all looked at him as though he was raving mad.

Amy Short was tapping away at the wall with her fingertips, feeling with her hands. With a sigh, she took a step back and reached into her coat. She pulled out an object smaller than her little finger and held it up to the camera. "This memory stick contains all the information I've gathered," said the journalist. "Evidence of a supernatural gang operating from this cathedral. I wanted to talk to you, before I publish. But I *will* publish, because it's my job."

"Right, I've had enough," said Dodger.

"Wait," said Luke. "Don't do any—"

"Too late," said Raziel.

When Luke turned around, Dodger had vanished.

"Last chance," said Amy Short. "Give me your side of the story, on the record."

"What are we going to do?" asked Aurora. "This is serious. If she publishes anything that names this location, we'll have thousands of crazies sniffing around."

"Oh, no . . ." said Evelyn, nodding to the screen. A black shape appeared behind the journalist, wearing a familiar top hat. Dodger must have taken the emergency stairs that came out under a drain at the edge of the graveyard. A good two minutes at Luke's fastest pace, but a matter of seconds for Dodger, who could move faster than the human eye could detect, if only for short intervals.

Luke watched as Dodger threw something on the ground and a cloud of white smoke rose around Amy Short's feet. She toppled into Dodger's arms, and they disappeared in a blur.

"What's he done?" said Luke, heading for the elevator.

"Don't," said Evelyn. "Dodger can handle it."

Her voice was sharp and Luke felt a flare of annoyance. "It's not my fault she's here," he said. "No one followed me. She could have been tracking any of us. She could have seen the funeral. I didn't even want to have the ceremony at the cathedral. I said it was too risky."

"Don't bring my dad into this," Evelyn snapped back.

Aurora put a hand on her shoulder. "We shouldn't be arguing amongst ourselves," she said. "We need to work out what to do. If the Immortals become headline news, it really ain't gonna help our case with the Council."

"She might be bluffing," said Raziel. "Until we find out what's on that memory stick, we shouldn't act hastily."

"Well, let's have a peep then," said Dodger, who had reappeared, brow beading with sweat. He strode across the room, clutching the memory stick in his hand.

"Er, what did you do with her?" asked Evelyn.

"Dumped her in the river," said Dodger nonchalantly.

Everyone was silent, then Dodger's mouth split in a grin. "I'm not *that* bad, am I? No, she's sleeping it off somewhere out of harm's way. Well, in a cab heading to her offices."

"You're unhinged, do you know that?" said Evelyn.

Dodger cocked his head. "Quite possibly."

"You really think this will satisfy her curiosity?"

"Nope," said Dodger, "but I got tired of listening to her. Besides, she'll be asleep for hours, so she'll definitely miss tonight's print deadline." He plugged the memory stick into the computer terminal. "Let's see what she's dug up, shall we?"

Amy Short had not been bluffing, but as they looked through the evidence, Luke began to feel less concerned. It contained several files. However, no single one was compelling. There were leaked Ministry of Defence reports about the helicopter escape over West London, including some shaky amateur footage of Luke's evasive manoeuvres. Then several witness statements about the crazy chase over the rooftop of the pavilion in Covent Garden. There was even a shot of Raziel's silhouette flying in the sky. To be honest, it could easily have been digitally manipulated. The stuff about the sewer trolls was all conjecture as well, and the grainy images of a malformed creature emerging from a storm drain wasn't going to convince anyone with a healthy scepticism.

"We're in the clear, I reckon," said Dodger. "Now, I'm starving. Who fancies Thai?"

"Hardly," said Evelyn. "She knows about this place. She'll be back."

"I might be able to dissuade her," said Aurora, spinning the chamber of her pistol.

"I think we should tell the Supernatural Council,"

said Raziel. "We will be stronger if everyone knows of this journalist."

Evelyn pointed at the picture of the sewer troll. "Let's go talk to Greb," she said. "Luke, why don't you stay here and start working on our defence? You've got all our exploits in your scrapbook, haven't you? Put together a case for why the Immortals are better left alone."

Luke frowned. "Why don't I come as well? We can work on the case together afterwards."

Evelyn looked at the others, as if asking for help.

"Maybe you should stay out of sight, kid," said Aurora. "Until the story about you and Adam blows over."

Raziel said nothing, but he avoided Luke's eyes. Dodger had moved on already and had BIOS searching for the nearest Thai restaurants that did takeaway.

Luke couldn't help feeling sidelined. His mind drifted to the tracker. *I've got other things to do anyway.* "Okay," he said, keeping his face impassive. "I'll be downstairs if you need me."

"You want prawn toast?" asked Dodger.

"No thanks," said Luke, as he took himself off back to his room.

When he got there, he closed and locked the door. "BIOS – tell me where the tracker is."

"Processing," replied the soft female voice. "Tracker

located." The screen blinked and Luke saw the red dot hadn't moved much since he'd last looked.

He saw his scrapbook on the table. Evelyn was right – it contained everything about the Immortals. That's because, since he was about eight years old, he'd been their biggest fan, desperate to be one of the team. He hadn't asked to be brought back. But after his reanimation he'd given the Immortals everything. He'd been the one who had killed Sanakhte, and Draka. He was Victor's son. And yet he felt as though he wasn't being listened to, like he was being treated like a child. He missed Harker's leadership, and he missed his father.

The case could wait. He had to go find Adam.

CHAPTER 6

Evelyn led the others through the maze of alleyways in the City of London, trying to picture where they were. She had to fight to keep her temper in check as she pushed past crowds of baggy-eyed bankers, and workers on their lunch. The address Greb had given Evelyn didn't make a whole lot of sense. It certainly wasn't private – a restaurant called Luigi's, right on the riverside, in the heart of the City.

"Maybe he's booked a table?" said Dodger, grinning. He was wearing his smartest suit, which was still quite grubby, and had been persuaded to remove his top hat so he didn't draw too much attention. He still looked conspicuously Victorian, but people probably assumed he was an actor on the way to rehearsal at a theatre.

"I doubt he would fit at a normal table," said Raziel, who wasn't very good at spotting jokes.

He was in his latest disguise of a bodybuilder come straight from the gym. Jogging trousers, baggy hoody, baseball cap. Aurora had opted for a tailored trouser suit.

"I think it would be the table manners that gave him away," she said. "Have you seen a sewer troll eat?"

Evelyn let them chat. She'd checked out Luigi's with BIOS before they left. Apart from finding it had a very low rating on diner satisfaction, it looked like any normal Italian restaurant. Of course, she'd memorised all exits and entrances, plus the surrounding area. There was still a part of her that didn't trust Greb at all. What if this had nothing to do with the Supernatural Council? It wasn't beyond the intellect of a sewer troll to organise some sort of revenge against the Immortals after their recent conflict. A trap was a distinct possibility.

Their route took them across the bridge, but instead of heading straight to their destination, Evelyn took a detour north.

"Where we going?" said Dodger.

"Something I have to do first," said Evelyn. As soon as she'd realised the trip to the meeting place would take them near to the Bank of England, she knew she had to go retrieve the cache of papers left by her father. The letter had been nagging at the back of her mind ever since Baines had shown it to her at the wake, and she couldn't wait any longer.

"Something more important than pizza?" asked Dodger, who hadn't had time to order his takeaway back at the base.

Evelyn didn't answer for a moment. Her dad had been very clear about the level of secrecy required. "Just Dad's affairs," she answered, and that seemed to shut Dodger up.

The entrance to the Bank of England was on Threadneedle Street. "Best if you wait outside," she said to the others. Aurora nodded and stood with her back to the doors looking out across the square towards the neo-classical façade of the Royal Exchange. Raziel crossed the road to mingle with the tourists beside the statue of the Duke of Wellington on horseback. As well as a seven-foot tall bodybuilder could mingle, anyway. Dodger sat on the steps sulkily, watching a kid eating a burger.

"I won't be long," said Evelyn.

Dodger's stomach rumbled in response.

She pushed through the double wooden doors and entered.

Evelyn remembered the old building, before it was

renovated in the second half of the 19th century. It had been quite dark and dingy then. The interior now was grand, with a vaulted ceiling and a floor inlaid with mosaic patterns. Light flooded in from the tall elevated windows, and the reception hall teemed with people in suits.

Evelyn walked up to the main desk, where a man observed her with curiosity.

"Can I help you?" he asked.

"My name is Harker," Evelyn replied. "I've come to access a private bank vault that belonged to my father."

The receptionist frowned. "I think you may have the wrong place," he said. "This is the Bank of England, not a retail bank."

His tone dripped with disdain, but Evelyn was not swayed. She knew her father would not have lied to her. She fished the key out and laid it on the marble counter.

"Perhaps it's you who's mistaken," she said frostily.

The man's face flushed red. "I assure you, young lady—"

A woman appeared from behind the receptionist. Grey-haired, aristocratic-looking. "I'll take things from here, Henry," she said.

She picked up the key, and her eyes flicked to Evelyn. "Please, follow me, Miss Harker."

The receptionist stared in astonishment as his boss flashed a pass over a scanner and led Evelyn through a security gate. The woman's heels clicked on the floor and she didn't look back as she spoke. "Forgive Henry's over-zealousness," she said. "He doesn't know the work we do for our private clients."

Evelyn followed, speechless. She expected to be grilled at any moment, to have to prove who she was, or that she was following her father's wishes. But her guide said nothing as they passed a bank of elevators and went through a door marked "Private – authorised personnel only".

It looked to be some kind of storeroom, with shelves of stationery and old computer equipment. The woman led Evelyn past the shelves and to the rear, where a strange pattern of wood and inlaid metal swirls a metre across decorated the floor. The woman stooped and pressed a manicured thumb on the central point.

Evelyn jumped back in surprise as the floor fell away, twisting apart like the petals of a flower to reveal a narrow cantilevered staircase winding downwards.

"Victorian ingenuity is astounding, isn't it?" said the woman.

Evelyn managed a nod as she stared at the remarkable engineering. The mechanism hadn't made a sound.

"Over time the Bank's mission has changed," said the woman, as if she was a tour guide. She began down the steps. "The currency figures we deal with now are astronomical – almost inconceivable to the human mind. Most if it of course is just ones and zeros, when you come down to it. Money moving between computers and never touched by human hands. It exists only in a theory that people buy into." She waved a hand as they reached the bottom of the stairs and were faced with a metal door. It opened to reveal a small elevator barely big enough for the both of them.

Once inside, the older woman looked blankly ahead until a red beam flashed across her eyes. The lift doors closed and they descended.

And descended.

Evelyn had no idea how deep the Bank of England vaults were located, but she felt sure they were several floors beneath street level. When the doors opened again, into a nondescript white corridor, she smelt the stale tang of recycled air.

"Of course," said the woman, setting off at the same pace she'd used upstairs, with Evelyn tailing after her, "there are some clients who value a more traditional service, and who wish us to hold things more precious than money." They reached a normal door, and the woman opened it but didn't step inside. "Your key will fit box 98, Miss Harker. I will be waiting outside when you've finished. You have my condolences on the death of your father."

Evelyn stepped inside and the door closed at her back. She realised she hadn't spoken a single word to the mysterious woman.

The room was floor to ceiling deposit boxes with polished gilt plaques on the front, a simple number engraved in each corner. Each box was about three feet wide by two feet tall – big enough for a holdall, or a few briefcases. There was a leather-bound desk in the centre of the room and a single chair tucked underneath.

Evelyn quickly found 98, which was conveniently at eye level. She inserted the key into a smooth lock at the top and turned it. With a soft click, the door swung open vertically.

She hadn't been expecting the vault to be full of jewels, or gold bullion, or piles of cash, but she was still a little disappointed to see only a small clump of papers, neatly stacked. Not even a disk, or a memory stick, or a cool invention. She took out the papers and went to the desk, sitting down on the chair.

Most of the papers were old – that was clear from the yellow spots on the sheaves. But the letter on top was not. It had been typed on a computer. Though her father had been at the forefront of medical technology until the end of his life, he had long resisted actually writing on a computer until the last year or so of his life. Still, the tone made it clear that the words were his.

My dearest daughter,

The pages herein enclosed once belonged to my friend Victor Frankenstein. To my shame, I admit they are stolen property, taken not while he was alive, but after death. In the normal scheme of things, they should have passed to his son, but ... well, nothing is "normal" in our world, is it?

During the months leading up to our reanimation of Luke, I dwelled for many hours and days on the best course of action. I weighed it against my honour and the trust of my departed friend. I still do not know if I made the right decision to keep these documents from his son. And though I am loath to do it, I pass that burden on to you. Look into your heart – your good honest heart – and come to your own conclusions.

Before you read on, I ask you – think charitably towards Victor Frankenstein, though your instinct might move you not to. He was a complicated man, driven by unquenchable thirst for knowledge at a time when God and men would have looked upon his work with horror. Occasionally, perhaps, he lost sight of what was right, in the search for what was possible. But his love for his family, and dedication to the Immortals and his fellow man, was always at the forefront of his heart. May we forgive him for what he did, though he could not forgive himself.

Your loving Dad.

Evelyn's heart was thudding. If the computer printout and the contents didn't make it clear, the final word hammered home how recently the letter had been written. Her father never used the word "Dad" until the final weeks of his life. Not until Luke was back. He'd worked so hard, for so many years, on the reanimation, that it was like he could finally be a father again.

Evelyn folded the letter and put it carefully aside. The papers beneath looked like they'd been cut from a journal of some sort, with yellowing towards where the spine would have been.

There was no preamble, or introduction about their provenance, but the first page was dated at the top. *Salzburg, 9 Feb, 1845.*

She began to read.

*

Twenty minutes later, Evelyn was shaking as she read the final page. Her throat was dry, and her cheeks were wet.

She tucked the pages into the bag she'd brought with her, and placed her father's letter back into the safety deposit box, removing the key.

She tried to heed her father's words, but couldn't. Victor Frankenstein was not a hero of science, whatever her father had said. She wished she'd never come here and never read the papers. She was angry with her dad for laying the charge upon her.

How could she ever tell Luke? What good would it do him, or *anyone*?

At least they had sent Adam away. With any fortune, they'd never see him again. If they did, Evelyn didn't know what she would do.

The woman was waiting as she said she would be, and led Evelyn back to ground level without uttering a word. Evelyn left the Bank of England by the front doors and found Dodger on the steps finishing a hamburger.

"Sorry, couldn't wait," he muttered. "Got what you came for?"

"Not really," said Evelyn.

Aurora came over with Raziel. "You look troubled," said the gargoyle.

Evelyn forced a smile across her face. They didn't need to know. Not yet, and not before Luke. What she'd read changed nothing, really.

"Let's go and find Greb," she said.

Luigi's had obviously had one too many bad reviews, because the signs in its door said it had closed down. Blinds were drawn across all the windows.

"Good job I ate already," said Dodger.

"Sure is," said Aurora. "If I'd had to listen to you whining for another second I might have overreacted."

"So what now?" said Dodger. "Where's the sewer fella?"

"This is definitely the place," said Evelyn, checking the card again. "I say we look inside."

"Want me to kick the door in?" asked Aurora, taking a step back.

"Way not to cause a scene!" said Dodger, twitching. A set of lock-picks appeared in his hand. "Here, let me try. Not a door in London can keep me out."

Evelyn touched the handle and it opened. "No need," she said.

The smell emanating from within was fetid, and for a moment at least, it chased all thoughts of Victor Frankenstein away.

Dodger pulled his collar over his nose. "Albert's ears! That stinks!" he said.

Evelyn tried to keep her composure. "Either this is why Luigi's didn't get many customers, or a sewer troll has been here," she said.

They edged inside. The place looked like it had been abandoned. Tables were pushed against the walls, chairs stacked. There were menus on the floor, and still drinks bottles behind a small bar. Dust covered most of the surfaces.

"Look around," said Evelyn. "Shout if you find anything."

Dodger went into the back, and Aurora pushed through a swing door into a kitchen area. Raziel found a set of stairs to an upper floor. Evelyn was alone for a moment. Her mind was a mess after the Bank, but she told herself to concentrate. The important thing at the moment wasn't Luke and the secrets of his father, but sorting out the immediate predicament of the Immortals. Their very existence was being threatened. They needed to speak at the Council.

But where was Greb?

She heard a noise, and it seemed to come from the bar. Peering over, she saw there was a trapdoor in the floor. It probably led to a wine cellar – most of the buildings along the waterfront had stores below ground level. As she watched, the trapdoor opened. Evelyn reached for the extendable fighting staff harnessed on her back.

A couple of three-fingered hands emerged, then Greb stuck his head out, and his snake-like tongue flicked up to clean his pale eyeballs.

"Good of you to come, Evelyn Harker," he said. "If you'd like to follow me . . . "

CHAPTER 7

The red dot had been stationary for some time. Either the tracker had somehow detached from Adam, or Luke's quarry was no longer moving. He threaded down a series of narrow alleys near the Bank of England, and found himself on Throgmorton Street, a cobbled single-lane road filled with shops and wine bars. Luke was clutching a regular smartphone like any tourist trying to find his way through the warren of streets dating back to the Middle Ages. But his was connected to BIOS, showing Adam's location. According to the device, he was almost on top of him.

He paused outside an ornate façade marked with various crests and heraldic symbols. A gilt sign told him it was the home of the "Worshipful Company of Drapers", founded in 1361. Luke spoke into the phone, asking

BIOS for information on the location. One of the twelve great livery companies of London, the Drapers' Hall was, amongst other things, a wedding venue, a meeting space for hire, and a photographic studio. Through an archway at the front he saw a neat landscaped courtyard with fountains and sculptures. It seemed an odd place for Adam to come, but the GPS signal – accurate to within 10cm – was clear. He was inside the building.

What's he doing here? Not sight-seeing surely.

Luke ambled through the gate, trying to look lost in case anyone challenged his presence there. Thankfully, there were plenty of other people taking pictures, tourists and parents with bored-looking kids in tow. None looked tall or broad enough to be Adam. Several doors led into the buildings around the outside, but one in particular drew Luke's attention because of the two dark-suited security staff in sunglasses guarding it. And sure enough, it was the wing that housed Adam's GPS signal. The guards had ear-pieces trailing wires underneath their bulging collars. Luke guessed they weren't going to let him simply walk past. Above, on the third floor, was an open window and shapes moving within.

"BIOS, can you give me a blueprint of the building please," he muttered.

A split-second later it was there, projected onto the

screen. Luke used his fingers to rotate and zoom, looking for another way in.

He found one. Almost tripping over a toddler, he headed back into the street and took the next alley along. Checking to make sure no one was watching, he launched the grappling hook up to the roof and let the retractable cable carry him four floors up.

So far, so easy.

He crossed the roofs, some modern, others much older, and reached the back of the Drapers' Hall. This side was still overlooked, but as luck would have it, the office building opposite was clothed in scaffolding and heavy plastic sheeting. Luke peered over the edge and saw that the third floor had a narrow balcony. Luke hooked the grapple again, and paid out the cable gently to lower himself onto the metal grate. Adam's dot remained stationary. A set of double glass doors gave a view into the room, but Luke pressed himself against one side so a set of curtains kept him from being seen.

The room inside was large – at least twenty metres by ten. Massive, grand paintings – mostly historic landscapes of cities and ports in oils – decorated the walls, and three resplendent chandeliers hung at intervals from the ceiling. The room was dominated by a long mahogany table and embroidered matching chairs.

Twenty or so people were having a meeting, and Luke saw at once that they weren't all human, and none of them looked particularly friendly. One was obviously an ogre. Luke had never seen one in the flesh before, but he'd seen enough pictures among his father's papers. Victor had speculated that ogres and trolls were related genetically, one having evolved on land, the other in water. The creature was about eight feet in height, with a broad sloping forehead and a flat nose. The main clue was the arms, which seemed about a foot longer than normal, dangling almost to the ogre's knees. The hands themselves were huge, though more slender than a troll's, with knotted protruding knuckles.

Apart from two identical women with pinched faces and hunched backs, the others were all men.

The head of the table was occupied by a gaunt figure, with wide cheekbones and pale skin. His lips were a dark ruby colour, matching his passionless deep-set eyes, and were the only thing about him that wasn't monochrome. He wore black from head to toe, and his sharp features made Luke think of a dagger in human form – a deadly weapon. Luke guessed he was a vampire. Even though he was indoors, he wore black leather gloves. Everyone in the room looked towards him. The man was speaking, and Luke's extra sharp hearing picked up a few Russian

words, which his brain translated automatically –
"business" and "attack". Then Adam stepped into view,
and Luke shrank away a little.

What's he doing here? Who are these people?

"Dmitri," said Adam, with a small bow. Everyone
seated at the table turned to face him.

The black-gloved man looked at him expectantly.
"Well? What news?"

Adam shuffled nervously, hands clasped in front of
him.

"I went to the funeral as you asked," he said.

"You made a spectacle of yourself," said Dmitri. "We
have heard."

Adam stiffened. "I made contact with the Immortals."

Luke was confused. *Is Adam some sort of spy? But the
bus accident . . .*

The man called Dmitri lifted his chin a little. "My
sources tell me that you ran away. There was a chase."

Adam bowed. "I am sorry, Master. My resolve failed
me. However, I was still able to gain access to their base.
You were correct – it lies beneath the cathedral itself."
Luke's hands were tightening into fists, and he felt
his face flush with shame. After everything . . . Adam
was a traitor. The others, and Evelyn especially, had
been right. Was it all a lie then? Even what Adam had

said about his father? "There are five of them," Adam continued. "Though I didn't have an opportunity to look around properly, I've seen they employ extensive security measures. It will be hard for you to—"

Dmitri waved a hand. "We have another plan in place," he said.

"Another plan?" asked Adam.

A thuggish looking security guard by the door touched his ear and nodded to the leader. "Positions, everyone," said Dmitri.

Adam looked round sharply, seemingly as bewildered as Luke felt. The people around the table all stood, and an assortment of weapons appeared in their hands. Some were swords and daggers, others were odd-looking bulky firearms or sticks crackling with electricity. The individuals moved to the edges of the room, out of sight of the guarded main door. The hard looks on their faces filled Luke with dread. It was clear that an ambush was about to take place. The ogre stood behind the door, flexing his massive fists. Only Dmitri had remained in his place, and Adam.

"Master, what are you doing?" Adam asked.

The door opened, and the sewer troll called Greb entered. Luke was about the smash the glass and warn him, when he spoke to someone behind him.

"I apologise for the protracted journey. Please, this way."

Evelyn entered the room, followed by Dodger, Raziel and Aurora.

"Welcome," said Dmitri, standing and spreading his gloved hands.

Then the security guard behind the door pulled something from his coat and hurled it at Raziel. Through an explosion of smoke, Luke heard a terrible groan. Raziel was on his knees, some sort of corrosive chemical eating into his stone skin.

Aurora blasted a hole in the attacker less than half a second later before three glinting silver throwing stars thudded into her back and she fell. Evelyn's staff came out in a blur, and crashed into Greb's temple, sending him reeling.

Dodger was a black shadow, moving so quickly Luke couldn't keep up. One moment he was beside the others, the next he'd appeared behind one of the hoodlums, snapping his neck. He tossed a metal cylinder, which bounced once on the table then popped, scattering a cloud of blue smoke over everything.

Luke kicked the window doors open and leapt into the fray. He headed straight for Adam, whose mask was half covered in the blue dye, eyes wide behind it.

"You liar!" Luke said.

"No! Brother! You don't understand!" said Adam, backing away.

Luke lifted his arm, ready to extend his lightning blade.

Then a pain unlike anything Luke had experienced surged through his body. He felt like all his bones were breaking at once. He fell flat on his face. As the pain throbbed across his limbs, he rolled over to see Dmitri standing above him. Luke saw now that the tips of his gloves were spiked and fizzing with sparks.

"One of the problems with having so many metal implants," said Dmitri. "You are rather a good conductor of electricity."

In the back of his mind, through the sickening pain, Luke wondered how this stranger knew so much about him.

He tried to stand, but Dmitri moved in, somehow quick and yet unhurried. He grabbed Luke by the neck, hoisting him off the floor with a single hand. Dmitri squeezed, and Luke's legs scrabbled in mid-air. The vampire was grinning, showing his fangs over his dark red lips. He was way stronger than a regular vampire. His eyes glittered, black with silver flecks, and a gaze that seemed ageless. There was no hatred in the look, just a kind of mild curiosity, like a scientist inspecting an organism under a microscope. A banal evil that told Luke the person holding him had killed a thousand times, indifferently, and no mercy, pity, or other compunction would trouble him.

As Luke's carotid artery was compressed, he felt his face filling with blood and his consciousness began to swim. This vampire wasn't wearing UV blocker, he realised. How was he able to be out in the day without it?

Dmitri pressed his fingertips into Luke's ribs and another bolt of current ripped through him. He felt as if his scalp was on fire and his eyes would burst. Then he was dropped in a heap on the carpet.

"I'd stay put if I were you," said Dmitri. "That's only half power."

Luke's vision swam as he watched the carnage. The twin women were in the air, beating pairs of bat-like leathery wings. *Harpies!* One had Dodger by the ankle and swung him, headfirst into the wall. Aurora Cage was on her feet, leaping over the table with the throwing stars still embedded in her back. They couldn't have known she was immune to silver. She kicked one thug in the temple, but then jerked and reached for her neck. A dart protruded from the side. She staggered, eyes rolling back, as three of Dmitri's men leapt on her.

Across the room, Luke saw a chair smashed to splinters across Raziel's smoking back. Someone had scattered a circle of salt around the gargoyle.

They know all our weaknesses, thought Luke. *This was planned from the start.*

Evelyn was still fighting, swinging her staff with accuracy and venom, felling anyone who got too close.

"Move back," said Dmitri, and his thugs obeyed. The vampire lifted a hand and opened it, palm towards her.

A pale purple beam of light hit Evelyn in the face. She dropped the staff and covered her eyes, stumbling backwards. *Some sort of high intensity UV ray.* Then Dmitri drew a thick-barrelled pistol with his other hand. Luke tried to stand, but couldn't. "No!" he cried.

Dmitri pulled the trigger and a stake shot out. It went straight through Evelyn's shoulder and pinned her to the wall. She screamed in agony. Even though Luke's own mind was clouded with pain, he realised that Dmitri wasn't trying to kill her – he could have hit her heart if he'd wanted.

"Tie them all up," said Dmitri, tucking the stake-gun away. "The helicopters are waiting on the roof. Transport them to the silo."

Chains were produced from beneath the table. *They were there all along*, thought Luke. *Is this the Supernatural*

Council? Are they trying to kidnap us? The pain under his ribs was fading, but he played weak, biding his time. Dmitri's thugs wrapped up the unconscious Aurora and Dodger, then pinned Raziel's wings to his side, staying inside the salt circle. The gargoyle groaned, but he had no fight left. Evelyn hissed and snarled as they bound her too.

A mohawked vampire, muscles practically bursting through his suit, hoisted Luke to his feet roughly.

"Wait!" said Adam. "You said you wouldn't need him."

"I changed my mind," said Dmitri. "He's going with the others."

Adam advanced on the vampire. "But—"

Dmitri clicked his fingers and the two harpies landed in front of Adam.

"It's you I don't need," said Dmitri.

Even without being able to see his face, Luke sensed Adam's shock just in the way his posture shifted. "I don't understand, Master. Haven't I served you well?"

"Exceptionally," said Dmitri. "And that is why I am releasing you from my service."

Adam looked at each of the harpies, as if deciding whether to try and push past. "But ... where will I go?" he said.

Dmitri shrugged. "That's not my concern. But don't come back, Adam, or I will kill you myself." He looked at the other Immortals. "What are you waiting for? Take them to the roof!"

No way! thought Luke.

He shot his lightning blade from his wrist, and with a flick severed the hand of the vampire holding him. Spinning away, he drove the shimmering blade through the man's massive chest. The creature's mouth opened in shock, then he melted into a tumbling cloud of black shadows.

Dmitri growled. "I warned you," he said, electro-nails fizzing blue. "Nikolay! Deal with the boy, please."

The ogre pounded towards him, and Luke brandished the lightning blade, ready to defend himself. Nikolay picked up a chair and hurled it. Luke swung, slicing the chair in two. One part flew past and the other struck him on the shoulder. Then the ogre reached him, and a massive paw-like hand delivered a blow to the side of his head. Luke smashed into something hard. Somehow he was on the other side of the room. The ogre jumped onto the table, and gripped his leg. Luke was powerless, tossed like a rag. He hit a bookshelf, pain exploding through him, and crumpled to the ground. As he rolled over, he saw the shelves toppling towards him and threw up his arms.

Hundreds of books pummelled into him, then the case itself slammed down.

"Stop! Please!" he heard Adam cry.

The bookcase was hauled off and Nikolay stood there, drooling. He lifted a foot above Luke's head, and Luke didn't even have the strength to protect himself.

This is it! he thought. *This is how I die.*

He closed his eyes and waited for the ogre to stomp his brain to mush.

CHAPTER 8

L uke heard a crack of wood, and Nikolay grunted. The huge foot came down a fraction to the left of his head.

The ogre staggered away, and Adam stood there, holding half a chair.

"Kill them both!" snarled Dmitri.

Adam reached down and grabbed Luke's arm, then yanked him up over his shoulder. Luke had no fight left in him.

The rest of Dmitri's people closed in. The door was blocked. No way out. The other Immortals had been carried away already.

"Adam, I will give you one chance," said Dmitri coldly.

Luke could feel the panic in the heavy breaths of the

93

man carrying him. *I have to go after the others before it's too late.* But Luke could barely move.

Adam turned and ran at one of the double windows. Luke struggled weakly as he realised what was about to happen.

"Stop!" cried Dmitri.

Adam jumped, and Luke braced himself.

They crunched through the glass, and Luke's enhanced vision watched the fragments exploding outwards. He felt shards slicing across his skin. Then they fell together.

The thud as they hit the ground knocked all the wind from Luke's lungs and rattled his teeth. He heard the snap of bone and Adam bellowed in pain. But then he began to run – an awkward, hobbling run. The world shook with every step, but the hands holding Luke were firm and Luke let himself be carried. He heard people gasping, blaring horns and screeches of traffic. Adam didn't stop, even though he was practically dragging his left foot. They crossed several roads, went down a cobbled street, then past some wooden hoardings. Then the daylight faded for a moment, and Adam suddenly stopped. He lay Luke down.

They were inside a deserted building. The interior was gutted – a building site renovation filled with tools, stacked wooden pallets and scaffolding poles. Luke was lying on several bags of powdered cement. Adam collapsed beside him.

"Are you hurt, Luke?" he asked.

Luke could see blood on his clothes, and his ribs ached where Dmitri's nails had delivered the electric shock. One half of his face throbbed, which he guessed was from Nikolay the ogre's right hook. Nothing that wouldn't heal.

Through the various levels of pains, his anger surfaced. "What happened to my friends?" he said. "You were working for that man – Dmitri. What does he want with them?"

Adam stared at the ground.

Luke reached out and gripped his shoulder. "Tell me!"

Adam shook his head. "I am sorry. I don't know."

Luke felt the cuts across his face tightening as his advanced metabolism began the healing process. "That's not good enough!" he shouted. "You lied to me from the start. Why should I believe anything you say?"

Another pause. "Because we are brothers."

He spoke the words with utmost sincerity, dousing Luke's fury. "If that's true, it makes it even worse," said Luke.

Adam was rocking back and forth a little. "It wasn't supposed to be like this."

Whatever was going on between the vampire Dmitri and Adam, those answers could wait. *I need to stay focused for my friends.* "Do you know where the helicopters are going?" Luke asked. "Where's this silo he's taken them to?"

"It is in Russia somewhere," said Adam. "That's all I can tell you. Dmitri only tells me what I need to know – nothing more."

Russia.

"Who *is* he?" asked Luke. "Why were you working for him?"

Adam wrung his hands. "He is – was – my Master. He looked after me ... as Victor should have done. But now he has also abandoned me."

Luke's hazy mind suddenly focused. "Abandoned you?"

Adam nodded. "Victor didn't want me. He forced me to leave."

Luke was stunned. It seemed so cold and heartless. He knew that in those days scientists had done things that were now considered unethical ... but would his father have simply thrown Adam out – a living, breathing person? And one who was so vulnerable.

"I travelled north," Adam continued, "and ended up in Russia. I was alone, and desperate. I took to crime so that I could eat. It's a long story, but Dmitri found me and took me in – he cared for me. I have worked for him since then. Until today."

The pain in his words was clear, and amid Luke's sympathy, he felt guilt too. If what Adam said was true, then Victor was partly to blame for making Adam what he had become.

"How long were you with him for?" asked Luke.

"Many, many years," said Adam. "Time meant nothing for me until Dmitri found me. He became like the father I never had."

"He's a vampire, right?" said Luke. "Why does he want my friends?"

"I do not know," said Adam. "He never told me."

"But you must have some idea!" said Luke, gripping Adam's arm again. "Please think! What is it Dmitri does?"

Adam shrugged helplessly. "He has many businesses in St Petersburg. He helps people with security for their shops and offices. They sell guns and other weapons. He has friends in the government."

"He sounds like a gangster," said Luke. None of this made any sense. The plan to capture the Immortals was well-orchestrated. "But why come all the way to London?"

"People fear Dmitri," said Adam, "but many love him too. He can be charming, and generous to his friends."

"I bet," said Luke.

"I do not know for sure," said Adam, "but I think he wants to expand his business into London. He has visited many times in the last year."

Perhaps that's why he wants the Immortals out of the way, thought Luke. *The regular police would never be able to stop him, but we'd have a chance. Still, why take them prisoner when he could just kill them?*

"St Petersburg, you say? Is that where the 'silo' is?"

"I do not think so," said Adam. "Dmitri runs his business from the back of a restaurant called the Arimov. I have never seen this place called a 'silo'."

Luke stood up. The cuts on his face had dried. After the fight with Draka, Luke had begun to take regular doses of the healing accelerants devised by Harker, as a precaution. They effectively gave his body the power of regeneration. Not quite as quick as a vampire's, but within a day the cuts would have healed completely.

"Can you walk?" he asked Adam, nodding at his ankle.

"Yes," replied the masked man. He too got to his feet, flexing his ankle. "But where are we going?"

Every second Luke wasted was a second his friends

were in danger. Harker had actually managed to get Luke a passport in the weeks after his reanimation, but he was pretty sure Adam would struggle on a busy, commercial flight to St. Petersburg. That left one option. A longer route, but more reliable.

"Dartmoor," Luke said. "Home."

The Stein Foundation was a three and a half hour journey out of London, and the taxi driver warned them that it wouldn't be cheap. Luke had handed over the Immortals' credit card, which seemed to keep him happy. He didn't even raise an eyebrow at the state of his passengers, and Luke checked from time to time in the side-mirror to see how his cuts were healing.

He tried to keep calm, but he knew with every minute that passed, Dmitri was getting further away with the Immortals. He could be taking them anywhere. The silo might not even be near St Petersburg, or indeed in Russia. Maybe the whole silo thing was a trick anyway – a diversion. He felt sure that Adam was telling the truth, so far as he knew it. After all, the creature had rescued him. Why do that, only to deceive him on this?

For the first hour, Adam barely spoke at all, at least not to Luke. His lips would move, muttering to himself, and Luke saw his fingers clenching in spasms as his hands rested on his knees. Then he took to staring out of the window at the passing traffic, or the houses, or perhaps nothing at all. Despite his betrayal, Luke found he couldn't summon any anger towards his father's creation – Adam was obviously deeply tormented, a prisoner of his own troubled thoughts. Eventually, Luke heard his breathing behind the mask slip into the slow regular rhythm of sleep. The giant twitched and flinched every few minutes, only to settle again.

From time to time, the driver would try to initiate conversation. He talked about politics and politicians (he didn't trust any of them further than he could throw them), about football (the players were all paid too much), about climate change (not convinced), about the state of the roads (a liability), about his holidays he had taken (his beloved caravan), about the holidays he'd *like* to take (anywhere but France), about his wife (hard work), his ex-wife (harder work), and his ex-wife's new husband ("He's welcome to her").

Luke nodded along, without taking much in. About half an hour short of Dartmoor, the driver had to brake sharply as another driver cut him up. He released a string of oaths which Dodger would have been proud of. Adam stirred to wakefulness.

"Not far now," said Luke.

Adam resumed his silent vigil, staring out at the grey scenery of the motorway, until Luke could bear his silence no longer. The taxi driver was singing along to an eighties rock song, and Luke turned to Adam, speaking quietly. "Tell me more about Dmitri," he said. "You mentioned he runs a restaurant, but you must know that's just a front. Where did he get all of his weapons from? I'm pretty sure they don't sell them to civilians in Russia."

Adam sighed. "I believe he has some connections with the military," he said, "but it is not something I am allowed to see."

Luke let that sink in. He could tell that Adam was keeping something from him. *I saw his reaction when Dmitri told him he'd outlived his usefulness. He was devastated.*

"You said Dmitri took you in?"

"Many years ago," said Adam wistfully. He volunteered nothing more.

The fare on the taxi meter ticked over seven hundred pounds by the time they took the exit off the main road onto the heather-clad moorland. The Stein Foundation had no sign – it was just a gated track in the middle of nowhere. You would have to be a very observant passer-by to notice the cameras hidden in the gate-posts.

The surrounding land was covered in wispy tufts of grass and bog, but among it were several other sensors and security features to keep unwanted visitors out. The driver pulled up, and a moment later, the gates swung open automatically.

"What did you say this place was?" asked the cabbie.

"It's just a research centre," said Luke.

Which was sort of true. The Stein Foundation, originally set up by Victor Frankenstein himself, on the site of his former home, did plenty of above-board, well-publicised research into things like GM crops, clean-water technology, and other environmental concerns. As the cab drove up the two-mile track, they passed tents and buildings dedicated to such activities. It was a private company in control of vast sums of money with outposts and satellite offices across the world.

But the Foundation, Luke knew, had a more secretive division, known about only by a handful of staff. Underground, in labs accessed through several levels of high security, was the weapons and supernatural facility. The Stein Foundation developed most of the Immortals' combat equipment and computer systems, plus carrying out research into supernatural phenomena.

The taxi pulled up outside a weather-beaten grey house – a holiday home Luke remembered visiting as a boy over a hundred and fifty years ago. Luke authorised the fare, including a handsome tip.

"Second longest trip I've done," said the cabbie. "Did I tell you about the time I took Sean Connery to Edinburgh in 1982?"

"Yes," said Luke, closing the door.

The cabbie waved cheerfully and drove off.

Dr Anna Pavlovic came striding from the house in her black wellington boots and country attire. She looked like the lady of the manor patrolling her estate, but Luke had learnt her slightly fierce demeanour was just a front. When they'd first met, it hadn't been a happy encounter. Neither trusted the other, and they'd butted heads until they uncovered the true enemy in their midst – the power-crazed Dr Fontaine, intent on reawakening the demon called Draka, who feasted on human souls.

"Luke!" she said, glancing at Adam. "Who is this?"

With the cabbie chatting the whole way, Luke had only had a few moments to fill Dr Pavlovic in properly, over text message. "His name is Adam," said Luke. "Is the plane ready?"

He didn't mean to be rude, but they couldn't afford to waste a second.

"As you asked," she said. "Has there been no news from the others?"

Luke shook his head grimly, and they set off together around the house towards the airstrip. The Stein Foundation had a private jet, as well as several helicopters. Luke could have taken one from the Southwark base, but it wouldn't have enough fuel for the journey to St Petersburg, and Dmitri knew that location now anyway. It was compromised.

Adam kept pace easily. His injured ankle seemed to have healed itself, Luke saw.

"We looked into this vampire called Dmitri," Dr Pavlovic said. "Found nothing. But the Arimov is owned by Dmitri Ivanovic. I guess they're the same person."

"That's right," said Adam, speaking for the first time since they'd left the taxi.

The steps leading to the front of the small sleek jet were down. When they reached them, Dr Pavlovic spoke. "There are clothes for you on board, and we've cleared the flight plan with St Petersburg. We've also been in touch with one of our partners there. It's only a small military research base, but they will come to our aid if you need them." She reached inside her coat and gave Luke a small thumb-sized object that looked a bit like a cigarette lighter, with a red button on top. "This is an emergency beacon. Three clicks and they'll come."

Luke took it, put it in his back pocket and smiled. "Thank you," he said, offering his hand to Dr Pavlovic. She took it and squeezed.

"Glad to help."

Luke climbed the steps with Adam following. He settled in the cockpit, and immediately went through the routine of initial flight checks, almost like muscle-memory, letting the information buried in his mind come to the fore.

"Have you flown an aeroplane before?" said Adam.

"Yes," said Luke. "But only once."

"Oh," said Adam.

"Don't worry," said Luke, fingers flying over the controls. "I might not have many hours under my belt, but my brain has been uploaded with all the relevant abilities. I'm kind of half-computer."

Adam stiffened in his chair. "But computers crash, sometimes, do they not?"

Luke managed a smile. "Buckle up, please."

He clipped his own seat-belt into position, then taxied out in reverse, swinging the plane onto the airstrip.

As he engaged the throttle, the G-force pressed them both back into their seats. And at two hundred miles per hour, he lifted the nose in a perfect take-off.

*

Dr Pavlovic was as good as her word. There was no problem from air traffic control over England, or as they entered European airspace. Luke tried to do a mental calculation on how far Dmitri would be ahead of them, given the top-speed of a chopper and the refuelling time. With the plane's speed advantage, he reckoned they'd only be a couple of hours behind the Immortals.

If he hasn't done something to them first ... if he's not doing something right now.

Luke tried not to think of things he couldn't change, but his mind kept returning to the pitiless look in Dmitri's eyes. A man used to getting what he wanted. A psychopath for whom others' pain meant nothing.

And while they were in the air, there was literally nothing he could do. *Dead time.* He set the plane to autopilot, and went to the back to change out of his ripped, bloodstained clothes. When he returned, Adam had removed his mask, fiddling with it on his lap.

"I owe you an explanation," he said. "I may have misled you in some ways, but most of what I told you was the truth."

Luke retook his seat, and made a show of checking instruments as he waited for Adam to continue.

"I do not recall my birth, if you can call it that. I do not remember how or when your father created me. If I had a life before that, it is lost." He paused, and Luke glanced across to see a faraway expression in his disfigured features. "My first memory is of being in a wooden cabin with Victor. It was in a forest somewhere – a single simple room with a bed and a table, but I knew nothing different. Each day my father would bring me food and water, fresh blankets and clothes. We would spend hours talking, or walking in among the trees. My favourite times were when he read to me – stories of adventure and love. I can still hear his voice now if I close my eyes."

Luke kept his eyes forward, on the clouds scudding past the jet.

"Often," continued Adam, "he would make notes in a book as we talked. I asked him what he was writing about, and he said 'You, Adam. One day I mean to show the world to you, and you to the world.' I grew excited about that day – the day I would see the things that the books spoke of. I was foolish to believe that such a time would come. Each night Victor would leave me in the cabin. Sometimes I was lonely, but I always knew my father would be back the following day.

"Until, one day, he did not return. I waited and waited. Night followed day followed night. I was confused, and fearful. I had always been too scared to leave the cabin by myself. Hunger began to gnaw at my insides. Eventually,

I could bear it no longer, and I left the cabin. Winter had come and in soiled clothes I wandered aimlessly through the vast forest, freezing cold, bare feet bleeding. One night there was a storm the likes of which I have never seen since. The sky flashed and cracked. Rain soaked me as I huddled in a weeping ball, wondering why my father had forsaken me. I cried to the heavens, begging him to come. He did not.

"And then came the fire. I was sheltering under a tree when lightning struck. I found myself trapped beneath a branch as it burned. My screams filled the night, louder even than the thunder. By some mercy, the pain snatched away my consciousness."

Luke looked at the man sitting beside him, weeping into his massive hands. "That's horrible," he said gently. "I'm sorry."

Adam breathed a heavy sigh. "Sometimes I wish it had killed me," he said. "That Victor had not made me so strong. It took me many days to recover. I survived by eating things I caught, rodents or worms, leaves and berries. I drank from streams. And when I came out of the forest, I found a town. People were terrified – they drove me away – but I learned to conceal my features, and with the limited speech I possessed I sought out Victor Frankenstein. I wanted to confront him, and to understand why he had abandoned me."

It was the most Adam had spoken since Luke had met him. He hung on every word, torn with pity. Adam spoke with such emotion and sincerity, he never doubted for a moment the truth of the tale. So far the picture emerging of Victor Frankenstein left a lot to be desired.

"When I found his house – a beautiful house in the mountains – I waited until night time and crept up to a lighted window," said Adam. "There I saw my father – our father – he was with a woman. He was playing the piano for her. They both looked so happy, so content." Adam swallowed, facing straight ahead through the clouds as they cruised at 40,000 feet. "I became angry in that moment, I admit – I wanted to hurt Victor. To hurt both of them, and make them suffer the same pain I had undergone. But then . . . then my fury left me, and I walked away from the house."

Luke waited a few seconds, pondering the story, confused. "But you took the necklace."

Adam nodded. "I returned two days later – to try again to find the courage to speak to Victor. There was no one at home, but the door was open. I walked around the house, taking in his life, how different it was from the cold dark cabin where he imprisoned me. I found the necklace in their bedroom and took it. I am ashamed of it now. I vowed never to return, and kept that vow."

Luke wanted to ask more – about the years after, and Dmitri – but the plane's sensors indicated it was time to begin landing procedures. Luke took control and eased the plane down through the thick cloud cover.

St Petersburg glittered like jewels scattered against the black expanse of the Baltic coast, bisected by a wide river running out into the bay. As they swept lower, Luke made out wide, grand avenues, the domes of great churches, and huge monolithic buildings. He made contact with air traffic control to schedule a landing at the city's airport. So far everything had gone without a hitch, but this was just the beginning.

My friends are down there, somewhere. Adam's story can wait.

Luke opened the channel to speak to air traffic control. "This is flight SF103, requesting permission to land."

After a crackle, the controller responded, telling them to set a course.

Luke did so, sitting back in his seat and trying to stay relaxed. But every nerve was on fire. They were entering Dmitri's territory, and their enemy thus far had been one step ahead at every turn.

He'll know I'm coming. He'll be waiting.

Luke knew he was stepping right into the lion's den.

CHAPTER 9

The pain in Evelyn's shoulder was bad enough. The flesh around the wound was behaving perfectly normally, healing itself, though with the stake still stuck inside her, every tiny movement sent shivers of agony through her torso. But it was the UV beam that *really* hurt. One of the guards sitting on the other side of a wire mesh fence around Evelyn was holding some sort of portable UV spotlight constantly on her face, not intense enough to do lasting damage, but making her skin feel constantly on fire, and her head pound. He was grinning the whole time, showing a set of discoloured teeth.

"The first thing I'll do when I get free," she said, "and I *will* get free – is rip your throat out."

His grin widened.

I just have to get out of these chains first.

The truck they were travelling in went over a bump and she gritted her teeth so as not to cry out.

It had been a four-hour helicopter flight, she reckoned, though her mind was still a little muddled from the fight in the Drapers' Hall. She'd had a rough idea they were in Russia, from the accent of the guards. Her brief view of the outside world, when they'd been moved from the military style helicopter onto a lorry with caterpillar treads, had shown a tiny private airfield with a few hangars, an ancient snowplough, and a lot of snow in dirty heaps. Her father had spoken Russian fluently, and for once she was regretting that she'd neglected that area of study. Martial arts had always seemed more useful and exciting.

Sorry Dad . . .

The other Immortals weren't faring much better. All were chained at the wrists and those chains were attached to metal hoops embedded into the vehicle walls. Aurora growled in her daze, her eyes half open, while Raziel lay curled up, burn marks scarring his stony skin, and a circle of salt and chalk runes keeping him enclosed and weakened. Dodger was fully conscious in his bonds, but the vampire's thugs had blindfolded him, and gagged him when they realised how much he liked to talk. Even considering their dire predicament, Evelyn counted that a mercy.

So it had all been a set-up from the start. Whether Greb was a full-time accomplice of the vampire, or simply working for him on a one-off basis, there was no doubt the sewer troll was in on it. Another name to add to her revenge list, if she ever got the chance to enact it. Evelyn tried to see through the cloud of pain and remember exactly what had happened in the meeting room. She remembered the leader – the gaunt vampire giving the orders. Someone had called him Dmitri, hadn't they? And the two harpies, and the ogre. She guessed a lot of the others were vampires too – not that she recognised any of them. All Russian, possibly. And what had Luke and the masked man been doing there?

But among all the other questions, the chief one had to be – what did this Dmitri want with them? The ambush had been audacious, full of possible flaws. If he was bringing them all the way to Russia, when he could have just killed them, there had to be a very good reason.

The truck's brakes screeched and Evelyn felt her weight flung forwards. She moaned as the chains held her and the stake in her shoulder stabbed a tiny bit deeper. If she didn't get it out, the wound might become infected.

A stake to the heart would have killed her immediately, but this could be a lot more painful.

The back doors were flung open, and spirals of snow gusted in. Evelyn shivered as the biting cold enveloped her. Several guards, all wearing white furred camouflage suits, lined up outside, all holding weapons which looked like modified Kalashnikovs – their barrels glowing purple. *Some sort of supernatural arms,* she guessed. Not that she was in any position to fight back. Of all of them, only Raziel had the strength to break the chains, and he was barely conscious.

The metal locks holding the chains in place all released as one. Three of the henchmen shouldered their weapons and gripped the end of the chain, then tugged together. Evelyn tried to stay on her feet, but couldn't, and landed with a flash of white-hot agony on her side. She and the others were hauled off the back of the lorry and landed with thuds in the snow. Dodger made a series of choice curses muffled by the gag as he landed on his head and flopped over.

Aurora, despite being semi-conscious, managed to stand for a moment, swinging her fists at empty air.

Evelyn scrambled onto her knees and looked around, squinting into the freezing gale. She began to shiver at once – vampires weren't good with the cold. As far as she could tell, they were in the middle of nowhere. Snowy plains stretched in every direction, though a smattering of pine trees lay along what might have been the banks of a frozen river. The only sign of any human presence was a single fence post sticking out of the ground at an angle.

One of the thugs barked an order. When no one responded he advanced on Dodger and jabbed him in the ribs with his gun. Dodger tried to kick him, and received a kick back, right in the kidneys. His hat flew off his head. He managed to spit out the gag. "Come here and say that!" he yelled.

"On your feet," the thug said with a heavy accent.

Dodger obliged. "Where's my titfer?" he snapped.

The guards all stood around, frowning at one another. "My bloody titfer," said Dodger. "Tit for tat – *hat*. You lot are slower than a two-legged tortoise."

The guard with the gun ripped off the blindfold. Dodger saw the hat at his feet, and managed to flick it up with a toe onto his own head, where it perched at a jaunty angle.

"Ta-dah!" he said. His mouth turned down in a frown. "Don't all clap at once, will ya?"

The guard delivered a brutal blow with his gunstock across Dodger's jaw, making the boy's legs buckle. Then he grunted and walked a few paces away, crouched in the snow and pressed something on the ground beside the fence post. A spinning red light appeared – rising up from the ground and half-covered in snow. It threw flashes across the snow like pale bloodstains.

The guard jutted his chin at the others. Two went to Raziel and gripped his chains, hoisting him up. Two others approached Aurora. She shook wildly, semi-conscious, and tried again to swing her chained hands at them, but the guards moved aside and trained their weapons on her. Evelyn stood of her own accord. When there was a chance to fight, she'd take it. But now wasn't the time.

With a grating sound, a large hatch opened in the ground beside the fence post, throwing off a slough of snow. *An underground bunker*, thought Evelyn.

She felt a barrel in her back, and began to move towards the hatch.

Dodger spat out a tooth as he got to his feet. "I'll remember that fella," he said, scowling. He struggled on his chains, but even the master escape artist wasn't getting loose. Evelyn caught Aurora's eye, but saw only a half-focused gaze. She'd heard the tranquiliser dart would have been enough to put a bull elephant to sleep. Which left only Raziel. He was stumbling, bent over. He had no salt circle keeping him imprisoned, but there was no saying how much it had weakened—

He lurched sideways suddenly, knocking the guard off his feet and into the snow. Evelyn heard panicked shouting from the others, weapons drawn up. Raziel roared and spread his wings, cracking the chains. He rose into the air. Purple flashes erupted from the barrels of the guns as Raziel flew above them.

Aurora pounced, landing on three of the guards and flattening them. Evelyn saw her teeth close on someone's ear and heard a horrible scream of pain. Next moment Dodger's chains, smoking slightly, fell to the ground, and Evelyn saw a stopper in his mouth. He was at her side in the blink of an eye.

"Hold still!" he said, pouring something from a vial onto her chains. The metal melted away, and Evelyn reached up, grabbed the stake and yanked it out. The pain almost knocked her to her knees. Dodger hurled a smoke-bomb at their feet, and green clouds of gas exploded over everyone.

As she recovered, Evelyn saw the legs of a guard a few metres away – the one who'd been shining the light in her face. She aimed a kick at the knee and felt the joint give. As the man fell, she fastened her teeth over his jugular and ripped his life away. His blood tasted good, and a new strength surged through her limbs.

Cries rose up through the smoke, and the dull smack

of stone on flesh. She jerked back as a metal stake shot inches from her face. Dodger whipped around, a barely seen shadow tugging the currents of smoke with him. Guards toppled as hands delivered jabs and hooks faster than any human could react. Then Aurora loomed towards her, mouth covered in blood and still in chains. Raziel landed, and Dodger joined the group. They stood back to back, facing out as the smoke cleared.

"I think we took care of them all," said Dodger.

But as the smoke cleared, Evelyn saw he was wrong. There were thirty or more, in snow-camouflage fatigues, formed up in a ring. More were emerging from the hatch in the ground. They carried a variety of weapons – batons flickering with electrical current, and bayoneted assault rifles, the blades gleaming purple.

"Get these chains off me," said Aurora, spitting out a mouthful of blood. "I say we go out fighting."

"Speak for yourself," said Dodger.

"Coward," muttered Aurora.

One of the soldiers tossed a grenade, and with a *poof* purple smoke exploded over them and drove Evelyn to her knees. For a few seconds, she couldn't see or hear. Her body spasmed, out of control, and she rolled onto her side.

Nerve agent, she realised. She felt completely sapped of strength.

An engine rumbled nearby and a large quad bike with caterpillar tracks drew up. The soldiers picked up Evelyn and loaded her onto a trailer at the back. It took four of them to get Aurora in too, but they couldn't shift Raziel's dead weight at all. They settled for tying him by chains to the back, looped over his ankles.

After a barked order, the quad bike headed slowly towards the hatch, dragging the trailer and the gargoyle across the ground. Now Evelyn was closer she saw that the door opened onto a steep ramp heading underground. They descended into a tunnel.

It was gloomy at first, and she made out rough concrete walls with lights every dozen metres or so. Eventually the passage levelled out. They took a turn, passing several steel doorways. The retinue of guards followed them in two columns. Dodger shifted beside her weakly. "Where are they taking us?" For once, there was no hint of a joke in his voice.

They entered into a cavernous chamber, several storeys tall, filled with giant vats, industrial piping and metal shafts, with two gantry balconies around the perimeter above them, manned by several guards. The quad bike stopped beside a double door with a reinforced glass panel. Evelyn managed to prop herself up on one elbow as the doors slid open. Inside there was no light, but her night vision adjusted quickly. She made out several figures sitting or standing against a wall. She felt their cold stares. The quad bike reversed and then the trailer tipped on hydraulics, rolling the Immortals into the room like sacks of grain. Aurora landed on top of Dodger, who pushed her off.

"Bloomin 'eck!" he said, gasping. "What's she made of?"

Raziel crawled into the room, with several weapons trained on him. The doors slid closed.

Evelyn climbed to her feet, wobbling on unsteady legs. The effects of the nerve agent were wearing off, but slowly.

The other prisoners – she counted about ten – were moving slowly towards them. "Heads up, team," said Evelyn. "We've got company."

Aurora bared her teeth in a snarl, and Raziel rose to his full height. Dodger tottered like a drunk.

Evelyn's weapons were gone, but she still had her hands and feet. She watched the men and women advancing. They looked desperate – clothes tattered, features gaunt. She wondered how long they'd been in here. But there was no mistaking the way they moved and the hunger in their eyes. She didn't need to see any fangs to know they were vampires.

"Wait!" she said. "I'm one of you."

The vampires stopped in their tracks. A couple spoke to each other in Russian.

Then a man with grey hair spoke in heavily accented English. "You may be a vampire, but your companions are not."

"No, but they're my friends," said Evelyn.

Another of the vampires spoke to the leader in Russian, and he snapped back before turning on Evelyn once more. "Hanna says you are the Immortals."

"Spot on, my friend," said Dodger.

"My name is Evelyn Harker," said Evelyn.

The name drew several exclamations from the other vampires.

"We have heard of you," said the grey-haired man. "And I am Josef Yelagin." He frowned. "But where is your father?"

"He's dead," said Evelyn softly, trying not to betray her sorrow.

"Then you have my sympathy," said Josef. "Not that it will do you any good here."

"Where the hell are we?" asked Aurora.

Josef shrugged. "Somewhere within an hour of Leningrad," he said, using the Soviet name for St. Petersburg. "But no one knows the exact location of Dmitri's compound."

"More to the point, why are we here?" said Evelyn.

Josef laughed, but there was no mirth in it. He glanced at some of the others, then spoke quietly. "Food."

Evelyn felt her blood run cold.

"What's that supposed to mean?" asked Dodger, fidgeting.

But it made perfect sense to Evelyn now. Dmitri's incredible strength, his powers far beyond those of a regular vampire ... "It means Dmitri is one of the Corrupted," she said. "A vampire that feeds on other vampires and takes their strength."

"I remember Jonathan ... your father ... speaking of them, but only long ago," said Raziel grimly. "I thought the Corrupted were a thing of the past."

Josef nodded. "They were. Biting another vampire is the most depraved act we can commit."

"A cannibal vampire!" said Dodger. "At least he won't like the taste of yours truly then."

Evelyn treated him to a harsh glare. "The Corrupted began as an attempt to cure themselves. They thought that by drinking small amounts of other vampires' blood they could reverse the curse, because one of the side-effects is to be more resistant to sunlight. Sadly, others are psychopathy, megalomania, and aggression."

"Like lawyers, then," said Dodger.

"Be serious," said Aurora.

"Dmitri's people captured us and brought us here," said Josef. "In the beginning, only one or two were taken every week to satisfy his needs. But his appetite is ... growing. And it's not just vampires any more." His eyes travelled over each of them. "He feeds on different sorts of supernatural creatures also."

"I'd like to see him try," said Aurora.

"Yeah, he might find we don't take kindly to being his *amuse bouche*," said Dodger.

The door cranked open and the vampires cowered back into the darkness. Evelyn turned.

Dmitri himself stood in the half-light, dressed in a long leather coat. Beside him were guards in body armour carrying stake-launchers, UV grenades hanging from their belts.

"Been hearing all about you, fella," said Dodger. "I've gotta say, you sound like a right nasty piece of work."

Then Dodger shot in a high velocity blur towards the vampire. Dmitri whipped out an arm, and before Evelyn even had chance to blink, she saw the vampire's hand closed around Dodger's throat. He hoisted him off the ground, so his legs were dangling.

"Nice try," said Dmitri, "but you'll have to move quicker than that, my friend."

Dodger's face was going purple.

"Let him go!" said Evelyn, stepping forward. Half a dozen stake-guns levelled at her chest. She stopped. It would only take one and it was over.

Dmitri eyeballed Dodger for a couple more seconds, then let him drop in a wheezing heap.

The vampire pointed at Josef Yelagin. "Him," he said, and four guards stalked into the room. The other vampires scuttled out of the way, exposing Josef. No one made a move to help.

Josef shook his head, pleading in Russian.

Dmitri's eyes fell on Evelyn, and he smiled horribly. "And bring the girl too."

CHAPTER 10

The bells of the Church of the Saviour on Spilled Blood chimed midnight, its dark silhouette of domes and spires looming over the Griboyedov Canal. Adam seemed to know where he was going, and had suggested getting out of their taxi a few blocks from the Arimov restaurant and scouting the area first. St. Petersburg was a fantastical city at night, sparkling and grand, with wide avenues, monolithic palaces and lithe bridges spanning the bay. Luke's internal connections to BIOS told him that the church got its name as the site of Tsar Alexander II's assassination in 1881 – a bomb had been thrown under his feet, mangling his legs and face, and fatally wounding him. He had died shortly afterwards in his palace. Luke glanced across at Adam, his face as unreadable as ever behind his mask.

The autopilot had taken care of landing, and to Luke's surprise the Russian officials had accepted their passports as if they were important foreign dignitaries, barely raising an eyebrow at the strange pairing of a seven-foot man and a thirteen-year-old boy. They probably thought Luke was the son of a rich businessman accompanied by his bodyguard.

"That's the place," said Adam, as they reached a busy crossroads, zipping with traffic even at this hour. He nodded across the street.

It didn't look like much – a black awning over a discreet entrance, with pale blinds blocking any view of the inside. A gold plaque reading "Аримов" (Luke's brain translated into English) was the only indication it was the restaurant, and to Luke it looked more like a solicitors' office. A row of black Range Rovers were parked outside.

"So do we just walk in?" asked Luke.

"Dmitri runs things out of the back," said Adam. "There's a password to gain access. I know it."

"Sounds like a plan," said Luke as cheerfully as he could manage. *A very bad plan full of risks.*

They crossed the street, and walked to the door. He was even less sure what he would do once inside. Find an office and look for any clue about the location of the silo was as far as he'd got.

Inside, a female concierge in an oriental-patterned dress looked up from her station. Luke wondered if she was a vampire, or had naturally pale skin. Only the slight quirk of an eyebrow acknowledged anything odd. "Do you have a reservation, gentlemen?" she said, in Russian.

Adam spoke a word back, but it wasn't a language Luke knew. The concierge smiled, and nodded towards a heavy curtain. "Please, go through," she said.

Luke followed Adam, noticing the subdued lighting of a dining room beyond. They walked along a corridor, rounded a corner, and saw two security men flanking the door, one almost as tall as Adam, and the other smaller, but with the build of a fridge on legs. Luke couldn't see any weapons, but both men bristled. The taller one folded his arms, while the other reached inside his jacket. Luke's pulse quickened, and he prepared to draw his lightning blade with just a thought.

"Is Dmitri here?" asked Adam in Russian.

The men looked briefly at each other, and Luke registered their alarm in slow-motion. As fridge-man pulled out a gun, Luke flung himself forward and swung a fist. It connected with the base of the man's skull and he dropped like a heavy sack. The lanky one sidestepped and drew his gun, but Adam grabbed the barrel and twisted it free, breaking the man's fingers in the process.

His other hand went over the man's mouth, stifling his scream. With a jerking movement, he broke the guard's neck and lowered him gently on top of the other.

Luke let out a long breath, ears pricked and watching the door. He expected someone to burst out at any moment, but nothing stirred. He glanced at the bodies on the floor.

"Did you have to kill him?" he whispered to Adam. "He might have talked."

Adam shrugged. "He would have done the same to me. Anyway, these are only – how do you say it? – *lackeys*."

Luke used his ocular lens to switch to x-ray vision, and stared at the door. Four figures, seated inside. One was huge. None of them looked to be restrained. *It's a meeting of some sort*. He put his ear to the wood, but the sound was muffled. He listened for over a minute, but all he got was "London" and a word that might have been "assault" or "attack". Without more context, his translation was unreliable. Were they talking about the kidnap? Or was this some other plan to move on London?

"There are four," said Luke, pointing at the door. "You take the two on the left, I'll take the ones on the right."

"Very good," said Adam nodding.

Luke held up his right hand and counted down from three with his fingers.

As he clenched his fist, he kicked open the door and jumped through.

The room was dimly lit by a single ceiling lamp. Luke saw a card table covered in green baize, vodka glasses and a bottle. In the middle was a large piece of paper with something like blueprints. Two of the men shot to their feet straight away, the third fell off his chair backwards with shock, a cigar falling from his lips. The fourth – the massive one – was the ogre Nikolay from the Drapers' Hall, who looked up from his cards with a look somewhere between boredom and anger. A formidable opponent. *Better take care of him myself.*

"Change of plan," shouted Luke. "You take three, I'll handle the big guy."

Luke hurled himself at Nikolay.

The ogre dropped the cards and snatched him in mid-air, quicker than Luke would have thought possible. He found himself flying towards a wall and threw up his arms. As he landed on the floor, the room was spinning. He turned to see three blurred ogre shapes pacing towards him, three arms raised. Luke shook his head and the image resolved into one. He ducked under a grapefruit-sized fist, and heard it crunch into the plaster behind him as he rolled away. Nikolay's hand had left a substantial dent right where his head had been. The ogre grunted and picked up a chair, then hurled it. Luke lifted an arm and the wood shattered against his implants, driving him backwards.

Through the splintered fragments he saw Adam in battle with the others. One was on his back already, out cold or dead, while another was fighting for his gun with Adam. The third leapt in with a baseball bat and clubbed Adam's back, dropping him to his knees. Luke wanted to help but Nikolay was picking up another chair.

As the ogre drew back his arm, Luke darted in, sending an elbow into Nikolay's midriff. The ogre gave a satisfying wheeze and Luke twisted, side-kicking to roughly where he guessed Nikolay's liver would be. The giant body folded with a howl of pain. Luke spun again, a sweep this time, and dropped his opponent onto his back.

Looking over, Luke saw Adam on all fours, rained upon by the baseball bat and an electric shock baton. But Adam managed to grab the bat, yank it free, and drive the tip into the stomach of the man who had been holding it. He dropped the other guy with a nose-crunching head butt, then stood, shoulders heaving. He nodded at Luke. "I think they are all alive still," he said.

Nikolay snarled and tried to stand, but Luke planted a foot hard on his solar plexus, and pressed him to the ground.

"Where's the silo?" he said.

Nikolay's bloated face cracked into a grin. "Nice try, but I will never tell you," he said.

Luke's anger flared and he summoned his lightning blade. It thrummed into life, glowing and fizzing.

"Where are the Immortals?" he said.

"Dead for all I care," said Nikolay. "They're nothing but meat."

Luke didn't know what he meant by that. He lowered the blade, close enough to Nikolay's neck that he could feel the heat. Nikolay kept his stare hard.

"Kill him," said Adam. "He won't talk."

"Yes he will," said Luke. "This blade is close to a thousand degrees centigrade. It will cut through your shoulder like butter."

Nikolay swallowed, eyes widening. "Dmitri will kill me if I say anything."

Luke slashed at a chair with the blade, slicing it in two, then waved it close to Nikolay's face. "I'm happy to start with your arms, or your legs," he said. "You won't bleed to death because it will cauterise any cuts as quickly as it makes them."

Nikolay clenched his teeth.

"Arm it is then," said Luke. He trailed the tip of the blade to the ogre's shoulder, and let it singe the stitching of his ill-fitting jacket.

"Okay! All right! I will tell you! It's on my phone in my pocket," Nikolay said in a rush. "Co-ordinates in the tundra."

"Adam," said Luke, not moving. "Take a look?"

His companion came over holding the electric baton and fished in Nikolay's pockets, bringing out a smartphone.

"Watch him," said Luke, taking it. "If he moves, kill him."

The phone needed a fingerprint ID, so he stooped to use Nikolay's index finger, noticing for the first time that the ogre had only four fingers on each hand, and they had three joints, rather than two like a human's. Despite the gravity of the situation, he couldn't help thinking about updating his scrapbook.

"So where are these coordinates?" asked Luke.

Shouts rose from the corridor outside, mingling with a woman's scream.

"Looks like we will all be dead soon," said Nikolay.

Five henchmen burst into the room, all brandishing specialised guns. *Too many*, thought Luke. Then Adam raised the electric baton and shot out the lamp, throwing everything into darkness.

The security detail began to yell in alarm, but Luke's infrared vision kicked in. He grabbed Adam's elbow, pulling him towards the only other door and grabbing the blueprints on the way. Muzzle flashes blinded him but he didn't stop as they barrelled through into a short corridor, double doors at the end. Praying they weren't locked, he slipped the phone away and shouldered into them. They swung open easily into a kitchen filling with more shouts, clashing pans and the smell and smoke of cooking food. Several chefs backed away as Luke and Adam ran between the prep tables and stoves and grills. More yells at their back, including "Out of the way!" and "Stop them!" in Russian. As they passed a huge rack of plates and crockery, Luke tugged it over behind them. The sound was deafening, but they both slipped through another door and out into the cool of the St. Petersburg night.

They ran along a deserted narrow alley, past a row of parked scooters and a blasting vent, then out onto the busy street beyond. Luke flagged the first taxi they came across and slipped inside, telling the driver to head "To the Winter Palace" because it was the only place he could think of in that moment.

By the time he was breathing normally once more, they were several blocks away, and despite several worried glances backwards, there was no sign they were being followed.

Luke pulled out the phone once more.

Time to find my friends.

CHAPTER 11

Evelyn stared at the row of stake-launchers pointed her way. Dmitri's eyes glittered.

If I fight now, I die for sure.

Two guards grabbed each of her arms firmly. Evelyn sensed Aurora bristle and shook her head. "No point you getting killed as well," she said.

The vampire called Josef Yelagin lowered his head in defeat as another two guards approached. But at the last moment, he lashed out with a fist, nails raking across a face. The guard dropped with a howl, but something whistled through the air and buried itself in his chest. A stake. For a moment, Josef looked down in shock, then his skin began to blacken and shrivel. In a matter of seconds, he was smoke.

"A shame," said Dmitri. "I was rather looking forward

to that one." His eyes passed over the others, then he pointed at the female vampire called Hanna. "Bring her instead."

Hanna backed away but the guards grabbed her firmly. Together with Evelyn, she was led out of the cell. Evelyn didn't bother to look back at her friends. She couldn't bear to see their desperation.

As the guards took them along the industrial underground passage, Evelyn turned to Dmitri, who followed a few paces behind. "You're a traitor to your own kind," she snapped.

Dmitri grinned. "So it's fine to feed on humans, but not vampires. A little hypocritical, don't you think?"

"We feed to survive," said Evelyn. "You do it for power."

"Perhaps I have a different definition of survival," said Dmitri. "The powerful have always preyed on the weak."

"You make me sick!"

Dmitri looked almost hurt for a moment. "Perhaps if you tasted it, you would change your mind," he said.

"I'd rather die," Evelyn shot back.

The guards took them into a room with bare-tile walls, a concrete floor and a single piece of furniture – a steel chair that made Evelyn's skin crawl, with manacles at the ankles and wrists. Dmitri nodded perfunctorily at Hanna, who began to writhe and wail as the guards dragged her towards the chair. A vicious blow to the back of her head made her still for long enough that they could fasten her down. Two parallel vertical plates swung round and kept her head in place.

Evelyn strained as well, but the guards holding her were supernaturally strong – vampires themselves surely. She wondered if they were Corrupted too, or simply in Dmitri's pay. If the latter, she loathed them even more. How could any vampire stand by and watch this horror simply for the promise of money?

Hanna was coming round again, fighting weakly against the metal manacles, straining her head from side to side, neck tendons taut.

"That's right," said Dmitri, gliding up behind her. "Get the blood flowing."

Hanna's expression was so fearful that Evelyn wanted to look away, but she didn't. She locked eyes with the woman she'd only just met, and said, "Don't worry, I'll kill him for . . ."

Dmitri's head moved quick as a darting snake and he buried his teeth in Hanna's throat. His fangs fastened there as she squirmed and clenched her eyes shut. Evelyn saw Dmitri's own throat swallowing and swallowing. After perhaps fifteen seconds, Hanna went limp. But Dmitri continued his gorging for at least a minute. Then he lifted his bloody lips away. His body jerked in an involuntary spasm and he fell back into the arms of his waiting henchmen. More jerking movements tore through him, and strange guttural cries came from his lips as his thugs struggled to hold him. *Has something gone wrong?* Evelyn wondered. *Is he having some sort of fit?*

But then the spasms ceased and his men stepped away. Dmitri's eyelids opened, revealing eyes completely black like pools of tar. "I feel … strong," he said, his voice at least an octave deeper than before. The black orbs turned to Evelyn. "But I am still thirsty."

A guard unlocked the manacles on Hanna's limbs and lifted her lifeless corpse from the chair.

"No," said Evelyn, as she was hauled on her tiptoes towards it. "No!"

But it was useless to fight and soon she too was fastened securely. Despair sapped her strength. She'd never been so helpless. And though she tried to push the thoughts of her father away, they consumed her. *It wasn't supposed to end like this, Dad. This wasn't supposed to happen.*

She sensed Dmitri at her back. "At least make it a fair fight," she said, hoping desperately to give herself a chance.

Dmitri didn't respond. She waited for him to sink his teeth into her flesh. *Any moment now.*

"Unless you're scared a Harker could get the better of you?" Evelyn said, trying to keep her voice from shaking.

Dmitri paced in front of her, stooping slightly so his eyes were level with hers. They had faded back to their normal blue, she noticed.

"Oh, Miss Harker," he said. "I don't want to drink your blood."

Is this some sort of trick?

"You don't?"

"Well, not yet, anyway," said Dmitri. "You see, I have far greater plans for you Immortals."

Evelyn didn't relax. Perhaps this was all part of some psychological torture to stoke her fear before killing her.

"At first, I just wanted you out of the way. You and your friends were a nuisance, getting in the way on my London expansion. My best people were having a meeting in a club there but you turned it into a bloodbath. All but one were killed."

The fight with Minnakht at Clarence's, thought Evelyn. Several vampires had been killed that day.

"Very sorry to throw a spanner in the works," she said.

Dmitri frowned in confusion.

"It's an English expression," said Evelyn. "It means I'm not sorry at all."

Dmitri's face tensed with anger for a moment, before returning to a state of calm.

"But it was a blessing, really," he said. "Another English expression – *Every cloud has a silver lining*. Once I knew what you were capable of, I had a better idea. What if I could *employ* you?"

"Ha!" said Evelyn. "I'd never work for you and neither would the others. If that's your plan, you might as well kill me now."

Dmitri rolled his eyes. "Perhaps employ was the wrong word. I should have said *control*."

Evelyn couldn't help frowning. *What's he talking about? Blackmail?*

Dmitri straightened. "Mikhail, here please."

One of the guards stepped to Dmitri's side. "Yes, sir?"

"Draw your gun."

Mikhail did so, and Evelyn braced herself. She wasn't going to back down.

"Shoot yourself in the leg," said Dmitri.

Evelyn wasn't sure if she'd heard right, but the guard pointed the gun at his thigh and pulled the trigger. The gunshot was deafening, and he fell to the ground. He didn't cry out or cradle the wound – his face remained curiously blank.

"Stand up," said Dmitri.

Without even a grimace, Mikhail got up. "Shoot your other leg."

Mikhail did so, and collapsed again. There was a lot of blood on the floor now, but if he was a vampire, he would heal in time. It was the emptiness of the guard's eyes that made Evelyn shudder. *Hypnosis.* Her father had told her about it once – it was rumoured to be a skill of those steeped in the Corruption.

"Stand up," said Dmitri again.

Somehow, Mikhail did so, but he was struggling to stay on his feet. "Okay, now shoot yourself in—"

"Stop!" said Evelyn. "I've seen enough."

"Very well," said Dmitri. "So now you understand my powers better. Of course I don't want you to think that all of my people are forced to work for me. I have many loyal followers. I cannot run my businesses with people who cannot think for themselves. But it helps having a supply of disposable muscle." Dmitri smiled. "And soon I will own the most formidable muscle of all . . . my own superhero hit squad. No one will stand in my way."

Evelyn felt the despair clawing at her gut again. "You can't control us. We won't let you."

Dmitri smiled. "Keep telling yourself that. Fight it, my child. But trust me, many have said those words, and no one has been able to resist it yet. Of course, you are all very different. I will have to adjust for your individual minds, but we still have some time." He looked at someone behind the chair. "Prepare her."

Evelyn was just wondering what he meant by *some time*, when her chin and forehead were gripped by strong hands. Some sort of mask was placed over her face and straps tightened at the back of her head. "Hold still," said Dmitri. "This won't hurt."

Evelyn froze, a sick fear rising in her stomach as clamps were placed over her eyes, forcing the lids open.

Dmitri reached forward and took her head in his hands, then drew his face close to hers. Black flecks shifted and swirled in his irises. His lips were still smeared with Hanna's blood.

"Let's begin, shall we?" he said.

Evelyn tried to look away, but somehow his eyes stayed within her field of vision.

"You cannot escape me," he whispered. "Free your mind and the fear will go. The pain will vanish."

Evelyn swivelled her gaze, but somehow felt his still. It was as if his eyes were tethered to hers, drawing her into the blackness, forming a connection that couldn't be broken.

"That's it," he said, his voice sounding like it was coming from inside her own head. "We're getting close."

His eyes clouded to black again, like they'd been flooded with ink. Her own vision seemed to collapse a little, darkening at the peripheries, shrinking so the room behind Dmitri became indistinct and shadowy.

"You cannot resist," said his voice. "I see your soul, Evelyn. I have it in my hands."

Evelyn felt as if she was floating. The chair under her had gone, and all she saw was the two black eyes, then simply black.

"Your memories are my memories," said Dmitri. "Let me see inside you. Show me your secrets."

Evelyn found herself thinking of Victor's papers. She saw herself reading them again, back in the safety deposit room of the Bank of England. The words on the page were clear. Even as she tried to escape from the memory, the images became clearer still. She felt the same shock as the first time, as if feeling it anew.

"How interesting," said Dmitri's voice.

Whether he released his hold on her a fraction on purpose, or whether he was momentarily distracted, Evelyn managed to break free. She tore her mind from the bank vault, and sucked in a deep breath of air. The tiles on the wall swam into focus once more, with Dmitri blinking in front of her.

"What a secret to keep," he said.

Evelyn's clothes were soaked with sweat. Her body felt drained, as if she'd run a marathon carrying a heavy back-pack. Even lifting a finger seemed almost impossible.

"You have a strong mind," said Dmitri, "but I've dealt with stronger. It will not be long."

"Keep trying, scumbag," said Evelyn, even though in her heart she knew it was an empty bluff.

"Take her back to her cell," said Dmitri. "Bring the stone man next."

CHAPTER 12

"Hey, chin up, kiddo," said Aurora. "You still with me?"

Evelyn managed to open her eyes, but the lids felt heavy.

"I'm here," she said. "How long have I been asleep?"

"Couple of hours," said Aurora. "Dodger's still not back."

The werewolf looked dreadful, slumped in the corner of the cell, her hair hanging in matted strands over her face. Her cheek was badly bruised and her lip was busted where she'd tried to fight the guards. Raziel was crouching beside her, head bowed.

But at least they hadn't been broken by Dmitri's hypnosis. None of them had. In a way Evelyn was glad – it meant they were still in control of themselves. But the longer they resisted, the more impatient their captor would become. That patience would snap at some point, and Evelyn had seen the brutality Dmitri was capable of.

If we hold out, we're just signing our death warrants. He'll kill us if he can't control us.

She stared at the door. "You think Dodger's okay?" she said.

"He won't crack," said Aurora. "He's stubborn as a mule."

The other vampires in the cells were muttering to one another in Russian. Two more had been taken since Dmitri started working on the Immortals and neither had returned. Everyone knew what that meant. They were merely food to maintain Dmitri's reserves of strength.

Aurora managed to stand up and slowly paced the cell. Evelyn had lost count of the number of times she'd done so, scanning every surface.

"There's no way out," said one of the vampires. "Don't you think we've looked? The walls are solid rock, the doors are steel. Even your human boulder wouldn't be able to break through." He nodded to Raziel.

"We can't just sit here and wait to die," said Aurora.

Evelyn racked her brain. *What would Dad do?*

The door opened, and two guards carrying stake-guns

stepped inside, training their weapons. The vampires scrambled back, shielding themselves.

Then a body was thrown into the cell. It was Dodger.

Evelyn rushed to him, worried for a moment he was dead. But as she rolled him over a groan escaped his lips.

"Dodger!" she said. "Are you okay?"

"Hunky-bloomin'-dory," he muttered, but his face told a different story. His eyes were bloodshot, his nose bloody. One of the guards threw in his crumpled hat as well, then the door closed. Through the small viewing panel, Evelyn saw Dmitri staring angrily before disappearing. Clearly Dodger had resisted too.

He coughed, and managed to roll onto all fours. "Haven't felt this rotten since New Year 1873," he said. "And that was a wild night, I'll tell you."

Evelyn was still looking at the glass panel. It was only about a foot square, and reinforced, but perhaps it was a weak spot. She stood up and went over, laying her fingers on the glass. It looked about an inch thick.

"Raziel," she said. "Any chance you could break this?"

"I will try," said the gargoyle. But as he tried to stand, he fell back again. Aurora went to his side and managed to help him up. Raziel hobbled to the door, then drew back his stone fist. The punch boomed through the cell, but the glass was undamaged. Raziel pounded again, and again, but each blow was less powerful than the last. In the end, he collapsed again.

"We told you," said a vampire. "It's hopeless."

"No it isn't!" snapped Evelyn. "You might have lost hope, but I haven't! I'm not going to sit here and wait to become food for that Corrupted slime ball. I'm going to break down this door and fight. And when it comes down to it, you can fight too, or you can die like cattle. Got it?"

That shut the vampires up. Evelyn didn't know if they could all understand her words, but the rough meaning must have been clear enough.

"Hey, kid – this might help," said Aurora.

She reached into her jacket and pulled something out. *A grenade!*

"Where did you get that?" said Evelyn.

"Managed to steal it from a guard on the way back from Dmitri's house of horror," said Aurora. "I was saving it as a last resort – in case he broke me. But hey, if we can go out fighting, I'm in."

"You cannot be thinking of using that in here?" said a vampire. "You blow us all up!"

Aurora handed Evelyn the grenade. It was a standard time-delay mechanism – the same sort of thing used in countless wars since the early 20th century. Simple but effective anti-personnel fragmentation weapon to inflict maximum damage on human flesh.

Evelyn looked at the glass panel. The vampire was right. The shrapnel from the grenade would have nowhere to go but across the cell. There was nowhere to hide. *Unless...*

"Raziel..." she said.

The gargoyle seemed to understand. "Very well."

"Everyone in the corner," said Evelyn. "As far from the door as possible."

Muttering and cursing in Russian, the vampires obeyed. Aurora helped Dodger over to join them, then Raziel turned his back on the door and spread his stone wings with a grimace, forming a barrier between the occupants and the door. Evelyn wondered how long it would take between pulling out the pin and the detonation. If she timed it wrong, she might lose an arm or worse.

"I need a shoelace," she said. "The grenade will have to blow right next to the glass. It won't even dent the door."

Aurora tossed over one of Dodger's laces, and Evelyn looped it around the grenade's lever arm. She tied the other end to one of the metal bars running across the panel, so the grenade was suspended beside the glass.

"Ready?" she said.

"Do it!" said Aurora, peering over Raziel's shoulder.

Evelyn pressed the lever gently, and pulled out the pin. Then she ran across the cell and took shelter with the others, counting in her head: *One . . . Two . . . Three . . . Four . . . Fiv—*

BOOM!

She heard a thud of metal on stone, and Raziel staggered. Her ears were ringing as she peered out into the smoke-filled cell. Then she rushed back out. Raziel's wings were smoking, dotted with embedded pieces of glowing shrapnel. "Go," he grunted. "I am fine."

Evelyn reached the door and saw the glass was blown out. With Aurora giving her a foot up, she scrambled through head-first. It was a tight-squeeze, but she eased one shoulder past, then the other, and dropped on the other side. Already she heard steps approaching – fast. Two vampire guards with stake-launchers rounded a corner. Evelyn charged. The first stake whistled past her ear, and the second guard hadn't even fired before Evelyn caught his chin and yanked it round, snapping his neck. She picked up his stake-gun and fired it through the heart of the second as he reloaded. He crisped up and collapsed into ashes.

From the remains, she took a key card and went

back to the cell. With a swipe of the card, the door was open.

"Quick!" she said. "There'll be more."

The vampires bundled out, looking around as if they could barely believe their eyes. Raziel, hobbling, came next with Dodger over his shoulder. And last of all Aurora. "Good work, kid," she said. Then she twisted, as something thumped into her arm. A wooden stake. The werewolf growled and yanked it out, turning to face a guard with a raised stake-launcher standing at the end of the corridor. She drew back her arm and hurled the stake, spinning through the air. It smashed into the guard's chest, knocking him to the ground.

"There are more," said Raziel.

Evelyn groaned as half a dozen guards hurried from a passage, wielding a variety of weapons.

The vampires from the cell looked at one another, their faces torn between fear and grim determination. With a roar, they all ran at the guards. A few fell quickly, killed by stakes, but the remainder stormed into the guards, biting and clawing. Evelyn turned from the carnage.

"Come on, let's go!" she said.

They rushed back along the corridor they'd entered by, and encountered no more resistance. Dodger was mumbling weakly on Raziel's back. Soon they reached the hatch and the key card did the job again. They clambered out into the freezing snow.

The truck was still there.

Aurora jumped into the driving seat and ripped off the panel underneath, then tugged out a collection of wires.

"Get in!" she shouted. "This won't take . . . "

The engine growled into life. Raziel climbed into the cargo area with Dodger, and Evelyn hoisted herself up into the passenger seat.

"Safety belts on," said Aurora, grinning. "Don't want anyone getting hurt."

Then she hit the gas and the truck roared off over the snowy wasteland.

CHAPTER 13

The Russian driver was pretty much the opposite of the London cabbie. He barely spoke at all, beyond refusing to take Luke and Adam to the co-ordinates on Nikolay's phone. He'd said he was finishing for the evening and it was too far out of the city. He dropped them on the outskirts, and after a walk in the freezing cold for about fifteen minutes, an old guy in a battered Lada had offered them a lift. He was heading along the southern highway from St. Petersburg, after working a shift at a rubber factory. Luke was grateful, but the man drove like a maniac on the icy roads, the rear wheels sliding dangerously as he leant over his steering wheel into the swirling snow squall.

Luke unrolled the paper he'd found in the card room. He'd been right – it was some sort of plan for a building.

A circular room, with corridors leading off at the four points of the compass. He didn't even know where it was, but they'd definitely been talking about London. Something about it seemed familiar, but he couldn't place it. There were no labels on the plan to give a clue.

The phone hadn't given them anything else either. Luke had disabled the security so it wouldn't lock its contents again, but aside from the co-ordinates, there was only a single number stored in the memory, and not much else. He guessed ogres didn't use smartphones a great deal.

"Dmitri will know we are coming," said Adam, looking across in the half-light. "You should have killed Nikolay."

Luke knew he was right, but it was easier in theory than practice. "I won't kill anyone in cold blood," he said. *Even a murderous ogre.*

"Your kindness is your weakness," said Adam. "People will take advantage of you."

Adam looked away, and Luke could only see the mask reflected in the dark window of the car. Behind it, Luke sensed a spirit haunted by sorrow, but Adam must have been angry once. At Dmitri. At Victor. All he'd tried to do was please, and everyone had let him down.

The driver reached a rundown motel and petrol

garage and pulled over. "I'm turning off ahead," he said in Russian.

Luke thanked him, and they climbed out. It had stopped snowing, and the cold hit him like a wall, snatching his breath away. It was a beautiful night, with a million stars against the black sky. Aside from the cluster of buildings beside them, and the string of streetlights snaking off into the distance, the landscape was bare.

Luke checked their position on the phone. The silo was about eight miles away, east-south-east, in the middle of nowhere. To get there, they'd have to hike cross-country into the wilderness.

"You okay to go on?" he asked Adam.

The giant nodded. "I have survived worse than this," he said.

Luke turned from civilisation and began to plod through the snow.

"You are cold," said Adam, about an hour later. They were walking along a snow-covered forest track, and the only sign of human habitation they'd seen was a wooden cabin, an upturned boat on a frozen lake, and the rusted carcass of a motorbike.

"Thanks for telling me," said Luke, teeth chattering.

His pain receptors were dialled way back by BIOS anyway, but even if his nerve endings were firing like a normal person, he was pretty sure he wouldn't be able to feel his feet any more. And there was no way back from a bad case of frostbite – once the flesh was dead, there'd be no choice but to amputate. They could probably have a go at replacing it using his father's old notes and technology at the Stein Foundation. But without Victor himself, Luke doubted the limb would function to as high a level.

"Let's make a fire," said Adam. "Warm up a little."

"We've got to press on," said Luke. "Another hour and we'll be there."

"Another hour and you will be a block of ice," said Adam. "Come, this way."

He didn't wait for Luke's response before veering off the path into the trees. As he walked, he gathered pieces of wood from the ground. When he had a handful, he found a patch of dry earth, and scraped some moss off the underside of a fallen branch. Luke watched in fascination, arms folded, as Adam whittled two sticks together until he had a wisp of smoke under the moss. He leant down, and blew softly. A flame caught quickly. Adam patiently helped the flames to grow with kindling, before adding larger pieces of wood. In a matter of minutes, they had a large fire, spitting and popping on tree sap. Luke moved close, warming himself luxuriously, while his companion sat a short distance way. He didn't seem to feel the cold at all but he lifted off his mask and let the firelight bathe his scarred face.

"Thank you," said Luke.

Adam nodded. "After I fled Austria, I travelled north. As far north as it's possible to go on land. I'm used to the cold."

The creature's eyes were wistful as he stared into the fire. Luke couldn't imagine what he had been through and all he had seen.

"How did you survive – you know, money, food?"

"I hunted at first," said Adam, "but I wasn't very good at it. Rats mainly. A cat if I was lucky." Luke tried not to grimace. "Then I begged, or stole, or scavenged. I found work for short times – logging, mining, and such – but something always went wrong. People fear a face like mine. I never stayed in the same place for long. Always moved on. I learned to fight because I had to." Adam lifted his massive fists and clenched them in the orange firelight. "And soon I learned I had a talent for it. It brought me enough to live on."

"You fought for money?"

"To survive," said Adam sadly. "I am not proud of it."

"So how did you meet Dmitri?" asked Luke. His toes were throbbing with blood again, a mixture of pleasure and pain.

"He found me in Murmansk many years later," said Adam. "I'd been working in the harbour, loading and unloading the cargo ships, but the overseer had told me the other men found me unsettling and he let me go. So I took to fighting again, and won of course. Dmitri was in the crowd, and came to me afterwards. He was the first person who truly asked me about myself, and who didn't flinch when he saw my face. Later he offered to bring me back to St. Petersburg, to work for him. I thought he was just a businessman. Only later did I learn the truth. What he really is. What he is capable of."

Adam fell silent, and Luke couldn't read his face at all. Was he ashamed? Angry? Or merely sad?

A thrash of guitar music suddenly filled the night, and Adam jumped to his feet, grabbing a flaming branch from the fire. It took Luke a moment to realise it was his phone and the song was Deep Purple's *Bloodsucker*. It had been Evelyn's idea of a joke to change his ringtone.

"Don't panic," he said, pulling it out. The number was one he didn't recognise. "Hello?" he answered.

"Luke? It's me!"

His heart almost burst out of his chest.

"Evelyn! Where *are* you? Are you okay?"

"We escaped Dmitri," she said. *"We're in Russia!"*

Luke grinned. "So am I! Close to Dmitri's silo."

"That's where we escaped from. We stole a truck. I'm phoning from a bar called Anatoli's outside a town called Zalrov."

Luke couldn't believe how good it was to hear her voice again.

"You're all there? Are you okay?"

"Just about. My money's almost gone. Can you get here?"

"Give me a second." Luke fished out Nikolay's phone and used the maps to locate Zalrov. It was only about five miles from his current location, but they were on foot in difficult terrain. "You're about two hours away. Hang tight."

"We will. But Luke, listen – Dmitri's more dangerous than we thought. He's Corr—"

The line went dead.

"That was your friend?" said Adam.

Luke nodded. "They got away from the silo. We have to meet them in a place called Zalrov.

Adam frowned. "They got away from Dmitri? How?"

Luke shrugged, trying to orientate among the trees. "I've no idea. We need to hurry – they're not far."

Adam replaced his mask. "You don't understand

Dmitri," he said. "It doesn't make sense he would allow them to escape."

"He didn't *allow* it," said Luke. "They're pretty capable, you know. Dmitri's not the first bad guy we've defeated."

Adam was silent, but Luke had an idea the mask concealed serious doubt.

"What?" said Luke.

"I am thinking that your friends are in more peril than you imagine," he said. "And we are too. We could be walking into a trap."

"You're just paranoid," said Luke, "but listen, it's time to call the back-up."

He took out the emergency transponder Dr Pavlovic had given him back at the Stein Foundation. She'd said they were based nearby, but he had no way of knowing how quickly they'd come. Still, he pressed the button three times and a small red light appeared. "Satisfied?" he asked Adam.

His huge companion was silent, and Luke wondered if he was even listening, or if he had lost hope entirely.

Aurora was helping herself to a drink from behind the bar, and under the circumstances, Evelyn didn't blame her. It was way after hours, and they'd found the place closed, but Dodger had picked the shutterlock with ease and they'd let themselves inside. It was a dump, with a sticky floor, stained tables, and windows that hadn't been cleaned for at least a year. It smelled of stale booze, sweat and desperation.

"Well?" said Dodger, as Evelyn put down the phone. He'd pretty much recovered from his ordeal in the truck, thankfully.

"We got cut off. He's here though, in Russia."

"And is he coming?"

"He said so, but I don't know how soon."

"Have a drink," said Aurora, taking down a second glass.

"No thanks," said Dodger. "I'm going to get some fresh air."

"Suit yourself."

He walked back outside, leaving the other Immortals in the bar. Evelyn went over to Raziel, and continued to prise the shrapnel out of his wings with a knife she'd found behind the bar.

"You know, that damn crook's not even said thank you for getting him out of there," said Aurora.

"I'm sure he's grateful," Evelyn replied. "You know Dodger."

Aurora grunted and swallowed another tumbler of

tequila. She'd found a shotgun behind the bar and it lay on the counter in front of her. It was the only weapon they had.

Evelyn looked at the clock above the door. It was almost six in the morning. Outside, the night was just beginning to give up its grip, with a hint of pale light on the horizon. She thought of her dad, and his cremation in the dawn. She missed him more than ever.

It was a stroke of luck Luke tracking them down. Well, not just luck. He'd obviously not given up on them. She remembered the last time they'd really spoken properly, back at the base. He'd wanted to come with her to the Supernatural Council, but she'd told him no. He'd looked so crestfallen and she'd hated herself for doing it. And then she'd read Victor's notes in the vault. The secret gnawed at her afresh. There'd be time to talk to him later. She hoped. And after that, no more secrets. She should never have pushed him away. It wasn't what her dad would have wanted, and it was bad for the Immortals. They were a team.

The door opened again, and Dodger came back inside. He was whistling to himself.

"Hey, Cage," he said.

Aurora looked up. "You look pleased with yourself."

Dodger pulled up a stool at the bar, and held out

his hand. "I want to say sorry," he said. "You saved my behind back there."

Aurora glanced at the hand, then at Evelyn. She raised her thick eyebrows, as if to say, *Is this really happening?*

Evelyn smiled and shrugged.

Aurora reached out to shake Dodger's hand. He moved lightning fast, and when Aurora jerked back, there was a pair of handcuffs on her wrists.

"What the hell? Very funny!" said Aurora. She struggled to free herself, but Evelyn saw panic set in on her face.

Then Dodger picked up the tequila bottle and smashed it over the werewolf's head. Raziel rose, but Dodger moved in a blur, and suddenly there was a ring of salt surrounding the gargoyle, and runes chalked on the floor. When Evelyn's eyes latched onto him again, Dodger was pointing the shotgun at her head.

"This might not kill you," he said. "But it'll make a real mess."

The look on his face was like nothing Evelyn had ever seen. Completely calm.

"What are you doing?" she said.

"What the guv'nor ordered," said Dodger.

And then she understood. They'd thrown Dodger back into the cell at the silo, and she'd thought he'd resisted the hypnosis like the rest of them. She'd *wanted* to believe. But Dmitri had cracked him. After all, he was the most human of all of them.

"You're under his control, aren't you?" she asked.

For a second, she thought she saw a pleading look in Dodger's eyes, but then it passed and he reached into his jacket and took out a vial. He threw it onto the floor at her feet and a cloud of green smoke enveloped her. Evelyn tried not to breathe, but it was too late. She lost all feeling in her legs and dropped helplessly to the ground. The sensation of loosening – of *weakening* – spread across her chest and arms and neck. It wouldn't be long before full paralysis took her.

Am I going to die?

As her vision began to cloud, she saw a number of figures in gas masks enter the bar. She knew their leader was Dmitri from his gait, and he crouched beside her, his breath rasping. With a hand, he reached out and stroked the hair from her face. Waves of revulsion passed over her useless limbs.

"Hello again, Miss Harker," he said. "Now, where were we?"

CHAPTER 14

From what Luke saw of it, Zalrov was a dump. An industrial town dominated by warehouses, factories and scattered tower blocks. As the sun rose he and Adam followed a set of overgrown rail tracks around the outskirts in order to reach the bar. They'd jogged the whole way to keep warm and save time. So far there was no sign of the promised back-up. *Perhaps the transponder was damaged in the fight at the restaurant,* he thought. *Or maybe they're coming from a long way off.*

In any case, it didn't matter. He wasn't going to let Dmitri capture his friends again.

Anatoli's was completely quiet, with the lights off. Luke wasn't expecting any different. The Immortals wouldn't draw any unnecessary attention. Still, the dead calm gave him pause, and he slowed his steps, checking his surroundings as he approached the front, past a couple of ancient petrol pumps. A couple of trucks were parked in the lot, but they looked like they'd been there forever, with grass sprouting up around the wheels and rust creeping over the front grilles.

The door to the bar was ajar a fraction, and Luke pushed it open further. Broken glass over the floor and a sour, stale tang of spilt alcohol. *Nice place.* He crunched over it. Something felt wrong, and he let his lightning blade extend. Then he saw Evelyn and the others, all seated around a table.

"Guys!" he said, heart slowing.

They looked up together, sullenly.

"What's up?" he said.

Evelyn's eyelids fluttered strangely. The twitch reminded Luke of something, but he couldn't think what. "Hi, Luke," she said.

"That's it?" said Luke. "That's all I get?" He glanced back to Adam, who remained in the threshold, looking around cautiously. "I know it took me a while to get here, but I thought you might be *slightly* more pleased to see me. So what happened to you? You're all okay?"

Evelyn's eyelids fluttered again, and suddenly Luke remembered. Greb had done something similar, back at Jonathan Harker's funeral.

Greb the traitor.

"Sorry," said Evelyn, more brightly. She stood up. "It's great to see you."

If Luke hadn't been on edge, the side-kick she sent at his head might have connected. As it was he backed off and it fell short by an inch.

"Hey!"

Evelyn's face remained completely calm. Then she launched forward and her forehead impacted with his nose.

The world went white, and Luke lost his balance, landing on the ground. He heard chairs being pushed back and strong hands grabbed his arms. Blinking through agony and streaming eyes, he found himself hoisted to his feet. Evelyn had one arm, Aurora the other.

"Let him go!" roared Adam.

Luke's huge companion stormed into the room, but Dodger suddenly appeared, crouched on one side. Adam didn't see the tripwire until too late and toppled. Raziel landed on top of him, a knee on Adam's back, and twisted his arm into a lock. Adam groaned as he was lifted up and pressed against a wall. It had all happened so fast, and it made no sense.

"What's going on?" he pleaded.

A slow clapping came from behind the bar as Dmitri

stood in the doorway leading into the back. "Hello, my conductive friend," he said. "That worked even better than I expected."

Luke writhed again, but Aurora had one of his hands in a wrist lock, and Evelyn was gripping a pressure point under his elbow to stop him extending his lightning blade. Both wore the same blank-faced stare. Luke had seen mind control before, but he never thought it could happen to his dearest friends.

"Snap out of it," he said to Evelyn. "It's me, Luke!"

"Hold him steady," said Dmitri.

They obeyed. Dmitri came out into the room, followed by several henchmen. He paused to look at Adam. "You chose the wrong side," he said, and punched him hard across the jaw. Adam barely flinched – just stared back defiantly.

Dmitri smiled as he arrived in front of Luke.

"For some reason Adam is immune to my hypnosis," he said. "I think it must have something to do with his strange physiology. All those ... *bits and pieces* stitched together like a handmade quilt. No matter, really, he was easy enough to control. It's simple really. You find someone's weak spot, and just apply pressure."

He lifted his hand, and the metal implants across his fingertips crackled with sparks. Then he touched his fingers to Luke's shoulder and squeezed. The electricity coursed down his spine, and Luke cried out in pain. After a short blast, Dmitri released him and Luke sagged in the grasp of his friends. When he could speak again, he managed to croak, "I always was ... a bit ... ticklish."

Dmitri sneered. "Your English humour never did work for me," he said. "Let's see, shall we, how long you laugh at me?"

He trailed his hand over Luke's chest then up to his neck. Luke tensed, ready for another shock. But instead Dmitri gripped his jawbone hard and pulled his chin up so they were looking directly into each other's eyes. "You cannot keep me out," he said, his voice a low rasp.

Luke stared at him, drawn to his strange grey eyes. As he stared, they seemed to darken as if they were controlled by a dimmer switch. "You cannot resist," said Dmitri.

The fear and panic in Luke's heart began to loosen their hold, his thoughts fogging over. It felt oddly comforting, and he forgot the aches and pains across his body. He felt like he was floating, somewhere warm, and it was because of the eyes. Their blackness welcomed him and he let himself drift on currents of untethered consciousness towards them. Then something snagged.

No ... he told himself.

He shook his head and cleared his thoughts. Dmitri's eyes brightened back to normal.

"Never mind," Dmitri sighed theatrically. "I would have liked you on our team."

"For your attack in London?" Luke said. *If we do get out of this mess, we need to know his plan.*

Dmitri looked moderately surprised. "Well, aren't you the detective?" he said.

"What are you going to do?" asked Luke.

Dmitri tapped the side of his nose. "I don't want you to feel left out, though," he continued. "You and Adam can assist with the weapons testing."

"What weapons?" said Luke.

"The Immortals, of course," said Dmitri. "My new toys." He walked towards the door and held it wide open. "You will have a minute head start. No, two minutes. Let's make this fun." He nodded. "Let them go."

Evelyn and Aurora released him at once, and Raziel backed off from Adam.

Luke stretched his sore arm, turning to his friends. "You're stronger than this," he said to them. "Remember who you are!"

"You're wasting time," said Dmitri. "In one minute fifty seconds, I'll give the order, and the hunt will begin."

The hunt? Luke looked at Evelyn and understood. *He's*

going to set the Immortals on us like a pack of dogs. Her eyelids twitched again, her eyes travelling up and left a second. *She's completely under Dmitri's control.*

The henchmen all levelled assault rifles, the tips of the barrels glowing purple.

Adam came to his side. "Luke, come with me," he said. "If we stay, we die."

"He's right," said Dmitri, checking his watch. "One minute forty."

Luke gave the Immortals a final despairing glance, then sprinted out of the door.

The worst part for Evelyn was the tiny part of her consciousness that remained, like a small voice screaming in the corner of a black cave. It begged to be free, but there was no way out of the darkness. It consumed her utterly.

She watched Adam follow Luke out of Anatoli's and prayed that he would run and run and not look back. Because she knew when Dmitri gave the order, she would go after him. She would track him down, and kill him, and drink his blood. She wouldn't stop. She *couldn't.*

At her side, Aurora was breathing hard, panting almost, in thrall to her wolf instincts. Raziel and Dodger waited.

Dmitri looked up from his watch. She watched his lips move.

"It's time," he said.

Yes, master.

Evelyn bolted through the door into the darkness, her vampire night-vision throwing everything in crystal clear relief. She scanned for her prey, scenting the hot blood from Luke's bleeding nose. Aurora was already running towards the undergrowth, and Raziel spread his wings and took off like a shadow. Dodger burst ahead in a blur of speed, his feet barely scuffing the freshly fallen snow.

Still the small voice screamed to be heard.

Evelyn ignored it and ran after her friends, plunging into the trees.

CHAPTER 15

T he hunt was on. Luke knew he and Adam didn't stand a chance.

The blood had crusted under his nose, and he wondered if it was broken. His heart thumped and his breathing was ragged as they charged into the unknown. His internal GPS told him the spruce forest covered several square kilometres, but it was safer than being out in the open.

Would the other Immortals really do it? Would they follow Dmitri's orders?

I'd rather not wait to find out.

He'd read once about vampires using mind control, but it involved drinking the blood of other vampires, and that was considered a deeply depraved act in vampiric circles. If Dmitri was capable of that, he was capable of anything.

Adam tripped over a tree root, and fell headlong. Luke went back to him, and tried to heave him to his feet. "Come on. You have to get up."

"Leave me," said Adam. "I am slowing you down."

It was true, but there was no way Luke was going to abandon his companion now.

"Get up!" he said.

As Adam clambered to his feet, Luke heard the sound of twigs snapping back the way they'd run.

They're coming.

With Adam at his side, he pressed on deeper into the forest. As he ran, he wondered what he would do, if it came to a fight. He'd have to defend himself but he couldn't kill them. But Adam could hardly be expected to have the same reservations. The Immortals were nothing to him.

He heard a bone-chilling howl pierce the night. Aurora's hunting cry.

The snow was making each step harder. His feet and trouser legs were caked with ice. He found himself thinking through the Immortals' abilities. Evelyn with her martial arts, Aurora with her bite pressure, Dodger with his chemical weaponry, Raziel with his indestructible body and incredible strength. They were the perfect hunting party – they had Evelyn's night vision, Raziel's aerial view, Aurora's nose and Dodger's speed.

We don't stand a chance.

Something whipped through the high branches of the pine trees overhead and Luke pulled Adam against a trunk. Raziel circled like a giant bat against the night sky and passed on.

Luke pointed east. His maps told him there was a river that way, leading to a lake. Water might give them a chance to kill the trail.

They'd just stepped out when Luke caught sight of a blur in the trees a hundred yards ahead.

"Dodger," he whispered, dropping into a crouch.

The figure stopped, breathing hard and scanning the trees. Luke knew that the lightning speed was only temporary. Dodger needed a few seconds for his muscles to recover between bursts. And eventually he would tire completely. Most of his enemies didn't last that long though.

Dodger's eyes latched onto Luke.

"Run!" said Luke. He tugged Adam after him. Another howl on the left flank, the sound of pounding feet. Luke adjusted his course. Dodger moved in ten-yard bursts, getting closer from the other side.

They're closing in. Where's Evelyn?

Suddenly the ground dropped away, and he lost his footing. They tumbled through ferns and bracken, bouncing and rolling. Luke curled his arms over his head to protect himself. By the time they rolled to a stop, he heard rushing water. The river was at his back, ten yards wide, deep and fast-flowing.

Dodger appeared at the top of the slope above, the one they'd rolled down. Aurora stood at his side, eyes glittering hungrily. Still no sign of Evelyn.

Something dropped like a bomb from the sky and thumped into the riverbank on the opposite side. It was Raziel. He stood, folding his wings.

Surrounded.

Aurora began to slide down the slope.

Luke looked back into the water.

"I can't swim," said Adam.

For the first time, he sounded afraid. Childlike.

"It's the only way," said Luke. He took hold of Adam's arm, and jumped into the water.

It could only have been the strength of the current that kept it from freezing. The cold was all consuming. Luke's chest clenched as he submerged, and his heart spiked in panic. He saw Adam flailing beside him. Then he broke the surface and gulped in a gasp of air. The current snatched them with incredible force and carried them with it.

Adam was splashing wildly, so Luke kicked towards him and wrapped his arms around the huge man's chest.

"On your back," he said. "Feet pointing downstream."

With a few more manoeuvrings, they positioned themselves floating side by side at the mercy of the water. Luke looked back and saw Raziel taking off. Aurora was crashing through the thick vegetation on the far bank, slowly but steadily, unconcerned about thorns lashing her clothes and skin.

The river narrowed around a turn, and sucked them over submerged rocks. Luke felt a bump on his legs but nothing serious. Here the trees grew right over the water, concealing them.

Adam had found a floating branch and clung on, using its buoyancy.

Luke felt a shred of hope. *We might actually get away...*

He cross-checked with his GPS. The river snaked for miles through the trees, passed through several towns before it emptied out into the lake. Luke focused on what looked like a set of buildings deep in the forest. They might be able to find a vehicle there. He was grateful for his reconstructed body – a normal human could never have survived in the water for long, but it was almost peaceful as they drifted at speed between the looming trees.

After a couple of miles, they reached the buildings, which had their own jetty. Luke realised it was an abandoned logging station, with a floating barge, corrugated huts, and old cutting equipment. They hauled themselves out, dripping and shivering.

Luke listened as he scanned back upriver. No sign of the Immortals.

"They won't stop pursuing us," said Adam. "I've seen Dmitri's powers. Once he has you, that's it."

Luke let the words sink in. "You mean the hold can't be broken."

Adam nodded. "Not while Dmitri lives."

"Then we'll have to kill him," said Luke.

Next to a hut, he saw a truck with a cracked windscreen that looked about fifty years old. He walked over, but his hopes quickly fell. All four tyres were flat.

Great.

"Above you!" cried Adam.

Luke looked up and saw Evelyn crouching on top of a woodpile stacked on the back of the vehicle. Her face twisted into a mask of feral rage, baring her fangs, and she pounced towards him. Luke resisted the urge to extend his lightning blade, and caught her mid-air. As they fell, he kicked out, hurling her backwards over his head. He came up to see her roll neatly and stand a few yards away.

She reached over her shoulder and took out her

extending fighting staff. With a couple of flicks, it was six feet long. She twirled it in a blur, then flew at him, jabbing and slashing. Luke let his super-quick reactions take over, but even with his ocular lens seeing everything at maximum slow-mo, he only just avoided the blows. Duck, step, lean. *Give Adam time.* The staff whistled past his head as she drove him back. Adam ran at her from behind, but Evelyn paused then swivelled and hurled something from her belt. A throwing star embedded in Adam's shoulder and made him stumble.

Luke extended his lightning blade at last and threw it up to meet her next attack. But Evelyn's staff was made of an enhanced metal alloy with an extremely high melting point, and the lightning blade bounced off it in a shower of sparks. He pressed towards her as they matched each other, blow for blow. Then he shoved her back, and attacked using close-quarter Kendo strikes. Sparks flew from their weapons as they clashed. He wondered if he could wound her badly enough to disable her. She'd heal, in time, if the damage wasn't too great. He aimed at her shoulder, but she twisted away, and spun low. Her staff took his feet away and he landed heavily.

She leapt into the air, angling the staff down. A blade flicked from the end, coming straight for Luke's face.

He rolled and the point sliced into the ground. She kicked him in the ribs and he curled up, unable to breathe. Then he heard her grunt.

Adam had his arm round her neck from behind, and hoisted her off her feet. Blood poured from his shoulder, but his forearms bulged with veiny muscle as he applied pressure to her throat. Evelyn's legs thrashed, kicking weakly. Her hands scrabbled at Adam's face as her own face started to darken. Adam squeezed harder, and Luke feared he'd crush her neck completely.

"Don't!" said Luke, standing up.

Adam paused. "She won't stop!" he said. "It's the only way."

Luke held out his lightning blade, advancing on Adam. Evelyn was barely moving in his grip. "I can't let you," he said, holding it at Adam's neck. "Let her go, or you die."

Adam's eyes were pleading, but he tossed Evelyn aside. She hit the ground, dragging herself weakly over the frozen earth.

Luke picked up her staff, just as Aurora appeared on the other side of the truck. Dodger came from behind, and Raziel landed too. They formed a wide ring, blocking any escape.

"Stop," said Luke. "You can still fight it."

Aurora drew her Smith and Wesson. Raziel clenched his clawed fists.

Luke shook his head desperately. "Remember who I am," he said. "We fought together, so many times. We saved each other's lives!"

Nothing in their expressions indicated they'd even met him before. Dodger drew two stiletto daggers from his boots.

Adam went back to back with Luke. "Let us die bravely, brother," he said.

I'm not ready to die yet, thought Luke.

Evelyn was on her hands and knees. As she stood, Luke gave her a blow to the temple with the butt of her staff, and her body went limp.

The others closed in. Aurora cocked the hammer of her pistol.

Then Dodger glanced into the sky.

Luke heard it. The *thud-thud-thud* of a helicopter rotor. Then the logging yard lit up as a bright orange flare fell to the ground, making them all shield their eyes. As it dimmed, Luke saw soldiers in black Special Forces uniforms leaning out, with guns trained on the ground.

After a second's confusion, Luke remembered the emergency beacon he'd pressed and realised with a wave of hope that the soldiers were from the military research facility affiliated with the Stein Foundation.

The helicopter hovered above the trees. Luke's eyes travelled to the highest building. There was some sort of chute conveyor leading to the top floor, near the roof. All that stood in the way was seven feet of werewolf.

Sorry, Aurora, he muttered to himself.

He brandished Evelyn's staff like a javelin and hurled it with everything he had. The blunt end struck Aurora in the chest, and knocked her back ten feet. "Go!" Luke shouted at Adam, before running and leaping onto the chute, beginning to climb. The metal clanged under his feet and Adam followed behind. At the top, Luke gripped the corrugated parapet and hoisted himself onto the roof. Adam struggled up after him.

The helicopter pilot adjusted his position, bringing the craft closer to the other end of the roof. A long jump, but Luke thought he could make it. He began to run, only to hear Adam cry out. Dodger, dagger in each hand, was darting around Adam, stabbing out with a dagger, as the giant spun around, trying to fend off the blows. Dodger's super speed ran out, and Adam caught his wrist and hurled him off the roof. Luke heard a thump, out of sight. Adam's forearms were dripping blood as he staggered after Luke. The helicopter wobbled a little, but maintained its position.

"Ready?" Luke shouted as he and Adam crossed the roof.

"Ready."

As they reached the end, Luke leapt. His hands latched onto the chopper's runner, and he swung beneath in mid-air.

But Adam had stopped at the edge, looking uncertain.

"Take us closer!" Luke shouted.

The pilot in the cockpit shook his head.

"Do it!" cried Luke.

They inched a fraction nearer, but Luke could see why the pilot was so worried. His rotors were already close to the tree-line.

"Adam, you're going to have to jump," Luke said. "I'll catch you!"

The giant took a step back, just as Aurora climbed onto the roof at the far end. She aimed her pistol and fired. A bullet cracked dully into the chopper's fuselage.

Adam threw himself off the roof. Luke let go with one hand and wrapped his fingers over Adam's wrist. He gritted his teeth as the added weight jolted through his shoulder and elbow. He heard another gunshot, then the helicopter began to rise. With a roar, Luke channelled all his strength into his arm, and swung Adam up beside him so they both had two hands on the runner. Adam was pulled up into the chopper, while Luke stared at Evelyn, as she watched him fly away, her face utterly blank. As they rose above the canopy, the trees fell away.

Just when Luke thought they were safe, Raziel's huge form climbed after them, wings flapping strongly.

"Go! Go!" Luke shouted, as the gargoyle closed in with astonishing speed.

Dozens of sparks danced over Raziel's stony skin and Luke was deafened by staccato machine gun blasts just over his head. Two soldiers were leaning out, training fire on the gargoyle. The bullets ricocheted off, but were enough of an irritant for Raziel to twist in the air and shield himself with a wing. The helicopter nosed down and soared away, leaving their pursuer behind.

Luke hung on to the runner as the trees whipped by beneath. He felt no relief or triumph.

They'd escaped, but what did that mean for the other Immortals? Dmitri didn't seem the sort to accept failure, or offer second chances.

Will I ever see my friends again?

CHAPTER 16

A soldier helped Luke clamber up into the back of the chopper. The two machine gunners were eyeing Adam with unease, but with the forest far below, Luke breathed a sigh of relief. He found a set of ear-defenders with an attached microphone, and put them on.

"We owe you our lives," he said in Russian. "Thank you."

The soldiers just nodded, and began to disassemble their weapons.

Luke leaned into the cockpit, where the pilot was flying. He looked terrified, and Luke guessed he hadn't seen a flying gargoyle before.

"What in God's name was that thing?" asked the pilot.

"Top secret military tech," said Luke. "A weaponised flying suit."

The pilot glanced sideways at him, not looking very convinced. "Where to now?"

For a moment, Luke was torn. His friends were still down there, even if they'd been turned into murderous thugs. There had to be a way to free them. But even getting close would be difficult.

"How many soldiers have you got?" he asked the pilot.

He shrugged. "This is it," he said.

"Four of you?"

"We got you out, didn't we?" said the pilot.

"Er . . . yes," said Luke. "I just meant, I thought . . . "

"Our orders were to extract you," said the pilot. "We've done our job."

Adam put a hand on Luke's arm, and brought his mouth close to Luke's ear. "I know you want to rescue your friends," said Adam, "but they are Dmitri's now. He has the upper hand. There's nothing you can do."

Luke didn't bother arguing. Adam was right about one thing – there was no way they could launch a counter-attack here on Dmitri's territory. The one advantage they might have was surprise. And at least he had a good idea where Dmitri would be heading next. He spoke to the pilot again: "We need to get to London."

The pilot laughed. "The Foundation doesn't pay us enough for that," he said. "The chopper has limited range. How about the airport?"

"That'll have to do," said Luke. "Just make it quick."

The chopper veered north, pressing Luke back in his seat. If they refuelled the jet quickly, he was sure they could get to London before Dmitri. For once, they'd be a step ahead, even if Dmitri knew they'd be waiting and even if they had no idea where he was planning to strike. The Corrupted vampire still held most of the cards – he'd had them up his sleeve right from the start, when Greb the sewer troll lured Evelyn and the others to the Drapers' Hall. The flickering eyelid was the tell – he too had been under Dmitri's hypnotic control, even at Harker's funeral. They'd been so busy worrying about the Council disbanding the Immortals, they'd never even stopped to think it might be a trap.

Luke remembered something. Reaching into his jacket he pulled out the blueprints from the Arimov. As he unfolded the papers to look at the plan, his eyes settled on the circular building. His heart beat a little faster, because now he realised why it was familiar. The four entrances, like a set of crosshairs.

"It's the same as Greb's ring!" he shouted.

Adam shuffled closer. "The troll?"

Luke nodded, and as the pieces slotted together, the dread began to build in his gut.

"I think we've found Dmitri's target," he said, stabbing the diagram with his finger. "This is the symbol of the Supernatural Council. Dmitri must be planning to attack it."

"Why?" Adam replied.

"It's where the heads of all the supernatural species meet," said Luke. "If Dmitri wipes them out, London will be his for the taking."

And he'll use the Immortals to do his bidding . . .

"Where is this place?" asked Adam.

Luke shook his head. "I don't know, but BIOS might be able to help."

"Who is BIOS?" asked Adam.

"You'll see."

Out of the window, Luke saw the sprawl of St. Petersburg appearing below.

The race was on.

Within three hours they were in the air again, and by six o'clock a taxi was dropping them outside Southwark Cathedral. BIOS would be able to identify the building for sure. If Luke could get word to the Supernatural Council, there was a chance they could organise an ambush.

Luke and Adam jumped the graveyard railings, and dashed towards the Tomb of the Angel. Luke hit the hidden button and summoned the elevator, then a voice behind them spoke.

"Careful now – I'll use this."

Luke spun round, lightning blade extended. A woman stood a few paces away, her arm straightened in front of her. It took Luke a second to take in the short haircut and the determined, delicate features of Amy Short, the reporter. Adam lunged towards her and she shrieked. A crackling, fizzling sound filled the air and Adam jerked, then fell to his knees. The journalist was holding an electric stun gun. "Oh my God! I'm so sorry!" she said. "Is he okay?"

Amy's eyes went even wider as she noticed the lightning blade for the first time. "What is that?"

Adam groaned, getting shakily to his feet, as the elevator door opened.

"You need to go," said Luke coldly.

"My colleague knows I'm here," she said, jutting out her chin. "You can't kill me. And you can't do whatever you did to me last time. I'll keep coming back."

Luke felt completely helpless. "What do you want?" he asked, letting the lightning blade retract.

"The truth," said Amy. "About you people."

She was still holding up the stun gun, and Adam eyed it warily. "Do not touch me with that thing again," he said. He towered two feet at least over Ms Short's head.

"Okay," she said. "But don't try anything yourself. I do kickboxing twice a week."

Adam grunted, and she put the stun gun back in her handbag. "Well?" she said, smiling sheepishly. "Are you going to invite me in?"

Luke weighed up his options. If he refused, it would only get worse, and he didn't have time to deal with any more reporters or police. But what would the other Immortals say if he let another stranger into the base?

Not much, at the moment.

"Come on then," he mumbled.

The three of them climbed in. "I'm Amy, by the way," she said as they descended.

"I know who you are," said Luke.

"And you're Luke Frankenstein," she said.

Luke tried not to look surprised. "How did you know that?"

Amy cocked her head. "It's called research," she said smugly. "The thing I can't work out is how you're still a teenager when you were born in 1848. You must have a hell of a skincare regimen."

The doors opened again into the main chamber, and their visitor gasped.

"Just don't touch anything," said Luke.

He tried to stay focused. Amy Short didn't change anything about the mission. True, it might get tricky in future, but the priority had to be saving the Supernatural Council and his friends. He walked to the central table, and placed the blueprint on the surface. "BIOS, scan and identify."

"*Yes, Luke,*" said the computer's cool female voice. The tabletop illuminated as BIOS performed the action.

"Is that Siri?" asked Amy. The journalist was turning on the spot, taking everything in. She lay her briefcase down.

"No," said Luke. "It's like Siri's older, smarter sister."

"*Without further inputs, identification is impossible,*" said BIOS.

Luke growled to himself. "Try again," he said.

"*Without further inputs, identification is impossible.*"

"Er ... maybe I can help?" said Amy. She wandered over to the table, reaching out.

"I said don't touch *anything,*" snapped Luke. Adam started towards her.

Amy lifted her hands defensively. "Okay, chill!" she said.

"Sorry," said Luke, slumping against a console. "You happen to have come at a very bad time."

Amy took out a Dictaphone. "Look, perhaps you could answer a few questions."

Snatching the device, Adam crushed it in his hands and let the fragments scatter on the floor. "Or maybe not," said Amy, a little pale. "What are you anyway? Zombie? Ogre?"

Adam reached up and lifted away his mask slowly. Luke saw Amy flinch, but to her credit, she stayed where she was, staring right at Adam's disfigured face. "I am a person," he said, replacing it again. "Just like you."

"But you're not like me, are you?" she said. "You're another one of this gang."

"We're not a gang," said Luke. "We're a *team*. We fight criminals."

"Is that right? Like those things from the sewers?"

Luke nodded. He'd no wish to tell her more than she knew already.

And none of this helps us. There has to be another way. Maybe if I go to Clarence's . . . talk to some of the other vampires.

Nope, that was a dead end. For a start, they'd never let him in on his own. And there was a good chance Dmitri would have moles monitoring the place – hypnotised vampires under his control.

"It's like getting blood out of a stone with you," said Amy. "Listen, I'm not your enemy."

"You're not our friend, either," said Luke.

"But I *could* be," said the journalist.

Luke didn't believe a word she was saying. "Adam, keep an eye on her."

He tried to think. Actually, Professor Tadic would probably know where the supernatural gathering was being held. The only problem was that his shifts at the Library were hardly normal office hours. Luke had no idea where he'd be at the moment.

"Just give me an exclusive. Tell me about your operation, and I can help you keep your secrets."

"By printing stories in your paper?" said Luke. "You'll have to try harder than that."

"It's not the story you need to worry about. It's the *angle*."

"No way," said Luke. "We're doing just fine, thanks."

"Really?" said Amy. "You seem pretty stressed actually."

Luke fell into glum silence. *I really don't have time to deal with this now.* "BIOS, search the digital archives," he said. "Look for any mention of a Supernatural Council here in London. Cross reference with sewer trolls."

After half a second, BIOS replied. *"Nothing in the archives."*

Luke thumped the table.

"May I?" asked Amy, timidly, gesturing to the blueprint.

Luke waved a hand at her. *There's no harm, is there?*

She peered closer. "This is a building, is it?"

Luke nodded.

"Any more to go on?"

Luke was silent.

"Oh, come on!" said Amy. "*Talk* to me. I'm not evil. I'm just doing my job."

Luke took a deep breath. They were at a loss, with no more leads. If Amy Short could help – though he severely doubted she could – he might as well let her.

"We think it's the location of a meeting that's happening soon – a meeting of all the most powerful supernatural entities from around the country. If it goes ahead, then it's likely that a band of Russian vampires, led by a hypnotic psychopath, will try and massacre them all, laying the ground to take over and unleash a wave of crime and death across the country unlike anything you've seen before."

Amy stuck out her bottom lip. "Riiiiight," she said thoughtfully. "Maybe phone the police?"

Luke laughed harshly. "The police won't be able to help. Nor will the army. You really have no idea what you're dealing with. If you try and fight Dmitri, thousands of innocent people will be killed, mind-controlled, or turned into vampires themselves."

"Understood," said Amy. "What about your friends? I know you have a werewolf."

"They're all under Dmitri's control already," said Luke. "It's just us two left."

Amy held the blueprint in front of her face. "This rings a bell."

"Seriously? BIOS is a supercomputer, you know that?"

Amy tapped her temple. "You can't put all your faith in machines," she said. "Sometimes the old-fashioned ways are just as effective. I'd expect you of all people to appreciate that."

"What are you talking about?" said Luke irritably.

Amy nodded to her briefcase on the table. "Let me review my files."

"No way," said Luke, and Adam stepped between Amy and the case. "You're up to something."

"And you're way too paranoid," said Amy. "Even for a teenager."

Luke glanced at Adam, but the mask gave nothing

away of the giant's thoughts. "BIOS already has all your memory-stick files," said Luke.

"That was just the highlights," said Amy. "My computer has ten times as much material. Seriously, that diagram – I think I've seen it before."

Luke nodded to Adam, who unzipped the case and pulled out a computer.

"Please don't crush it," said Amy.

Luke walked over, and booted up the laptop. A password screen came up. He looked to Amy, and cocked an eyebrow.

"Do I get an exclusive?"

Luke sighed. What did it matter, now? "If you can identify that building, yes."

"*Fluffypaws*," said Amy, blushing, then added: "My cat."

Luke entered the password, and the screen threw up a picture of what he assumed was Amy Short's pet, sitting on her lap. He followed her instructions to open up a series of folders, until finally he reached one labelled "River Sightings". Inside was another folder called "Bazalgette."

"Joseph Bazalgette drew up the plans for London's sewerage system in the middle of the 19th century," said Amy.

"I know that," said Luke. "I was around, remember?"

Amy smiled sarcastically as she opened the folder, revealing dozens of pdfs. "Yes, but did you know that many of the tunnels he built never got used, and were sealed off? They don't appear on the official drawings. In fact, the only place they existed, until yours truly sought them out, were in the City of London's Guildhall Library." Luke looked at her blankly. "I thought not." She nodded at the screen. "Open the ones labelled 'Redundant'."

Luke did as she said, which displayed complex blue-print images on faded paper.

"I was trying to track those sewer creatures," said Amy, as Luke clicked through the graphics. His eyes were immediately drawn to a corner section on the third page. He zoomed in.

"Bingo!" said Amy Short, brushing her hands together.

The circular chamber with four access points. The sheet was labelled "Westminster section", and followed by a set of numbers. *Latitude and Longitude.* "BIOS, interface with the laptop and find out exactly where that is," said Luke.

BIOS immediately displayed an aerial map of London, then zoomed to 1000ft elevation and overlaid a transparent version of the blueprint. The circular chamber was right beneath a vast riverside building.

"Oh my," said Amy. "It's the Houses of Parliament."

Luke frowned to himself. *The Supernatural Council are meeting directly underneath the human equivalent. I don't like the sound of that.* "We have to go now," he said, running back towards the elevator. Adam joined him.

"I'm coming with you!" said Amy.

"No chance," said Luke. "You stay here. It's too dangerous."

Adam blocked her with a huge hand as she tried to climb in as well. He patted her down, then took out her smartphone and crunched it to scrap metal in his hand.

"Hey! That's expensive," she cried. "You can't leave me here! You wouldn't even have found the place if it weren't for me."

"BIOS, place the facility on lockdown. Keep her in the main chamber."

Amy scowled. "You owe me an interview," she said. "The best interview in the history of—"

But the elevator doors cut her off.

CHAPTER 17

Most people moved out of the way quickly as Evelyn followed Dmitri and his men through the passageways of Westminster Tube Station. Those that didn't were barged aside unceremoniously. Aurora and Raziel walked on the flanks, staring straight ahead. Dodger hurried at Evelyn's side. No one talked. No one needed to. They knew the schedule exactly. Their master had made his instructions clear, and his will coursed through Evelyn's veins. She thought of nothing else.

At a junction of corridors, the group veered from the crowds through a door marked "Authorised personnel only". Inside was an empty passage. They walked a few dozen yards then stopped at a metal door. One of the vampires tried it, and found it locked. Dodger moved to the front, took out his selection of picks, and had it open in less than twenty seconds. The dark room was flooded with light. Circuit boxes on the walls. Spiders' webs. Stale air, and in the floor, a manhole cover. A crowbar was produced and Aurora prised it open. Evelyn made out the steel rungs of a ladder descending into utter blackness that even her eyes couldn't completely penetrate.

Dmitri looked at his watch, a little impatiently, then clanking sounds came from the shaft.

A sewer troll's head appeared, wearing a leering grin. The old Evelyn, pushed way back in her consciousness, recognised him. His name was Greb. He was one of them.

"Greetings, Master," he said.

"Take us to the Council," said Dmitri.

Of all the people on Westminster Bridge – the pacing commuters, the dawdling tourists, the workmen, the cyclists, the cab drivers, the delivery vans – only two were still. Luke and Adam stood on the north side, with the Houses of Parliament at their backs and the London Eye wheeling ahead, a little further up the river.

Luke looked at the diagram in his hand, then into the choppy brown waters below. *There!* It was an old storm drain emptying into the river about twenty feet up from the bridge. A dark semi-circle covered by a metal grate, half-submerged. He could sense Adam's fear in his stiff posture. Jumping into the Thames was a bad idea at the best of times. Doing so when you couldn't swim was foolhardy in the extreme.

"You don't have to come," he said to Adam.

"I will not leave you, brother," said his companion. Luke was glad – he didn't fancy facing the hypnotised Immortals and Dmitri alone.

They hurried off the bridge, pushing past more pedestrians. It was slightly quieter on the riverside path, but they would still be seen if they tried to enter the water. And the last thing they needed was the marine rescue or the police interfering. Luke spotted a section of the bank a few metres away, cordoned by workmen's cones and hoardings where they'd opened up a section of the riverside path.

Perfect.

"This way," he said to Adam, and they walked up to the sectioned off area. They were visible to people on the opposite bank, but it was getting dark. And by the time anyone raised the alarm, it would be too late. Luke threw his leg over the railings at the water's edge and Adam did the same.

They dropped into the water with a splash. Luke tried not to swallow any. Immortal he might be, but there were probably enough nasty bacteria in the Thames to seriously challenge *anyone's* immune system. Adam went under and came up spluttering. Luke reached over and gripped his shoulder. "Kick your feet like a frog," he said. "It's called treading water."

Gradually, with a good deal of splashing, Adam began to clumsily stay afloat.

Luke swam upriver towards the grate, and Adam came after him, holding the slimy wall to guide himself. They reached the grate in a few seconds, with Luke looking up every so often to check if they'd been seen. *In the clear, so far.*

He tugged at the grate until his shoulders felt ready to burst from their sockets, with no luck. "Help me!" he gasped. "We have to get through!"

Adam joined him, bracing a foot either side of the drain opening. It shifted with a grating squeal, and they tore it loose and let it sink into the river's depths.

They crawled on their hands and knees, through the scummy water, into darkness. The smell wasn't as bad as Luke expected. Musty, stale, and slightly organic. It was a couple of degrees colder than outside, like entering a cave. They reached a junction of channels after a few metres. Luke took the waterproof head-torch from his satchel and fastened it on. He illuminated the map again, just to be sure. "This way," he muttered to Adam, starting down a taller, dry shaft. They could stand, although Adam was stooping. Moss covered the slick brickwork in patches, with a pale tide-mark a foot off the ground.

It was only a couple of hundred feet to reach the Council Chamber and they hadn't gone far when Luke heard the chatter of voices. He paused, pricking his ears. They didn't sound raised, or alarmed.

Perhaps we're not too late.

As they rounded a corner, something dropped from the ceiling with a sticky sound. A sewer troll, on all fours. It straightened in front of them, head brushing the ceiling. If Greb had been telling the truth, the sewer trolls were guardians of the Council. *But this one could be working for Dmitri too.* "What you doing here?" it squelched. In the confines of the tunnel, the fishy stench of its breath was overpowering.

"Attending the Council, of course," said Luke.

The troll's eyes travelled to Luke's finger. "Where's your ring?"

Luke lifted his hand in front on him. "Darn it! Must have forgotten. Adam, show him yours."

Adam's mask-clad face turned to him, obviously confused. "*Show* him?" he asked.

"Yeah, your hand. Show him *really* close – it's dark in here."

"Oh," said Adam. He stepped forward and punched the sewer troll in the jaw. The huge creature wobbled, then fell flat on his back. Adam let his hands hang at his side. "That is what you intended, is it not?"

"Perfect," said Luke.

They stepped over the troll, and rounded a corner where the voices were louder. Ahead was a large doorway, and inside, lit by oil lamps, Luke saw dozens of people gathered in a circular room. *That's it – the Council gathering!*

He began to walk towards it, already feeling guilty about the unconscious troll. Still, the other members would understand when he explained everything to them. They could organise a counter-ambush, ready for when Dmitri arrived. If they could kill the Corrupted vampire quickly, then the Immortals would be released from the hypnosis. At least, Luke hoped so.

He was a few feet from the door when he heard a raised voice on the other side. "Who are you?" It wasn't addressing him, but someone inside the chamber. "You can't be here with all these companions."

Luke quickened his step, and saw Nikolay through the doorway at the far side of the room, holding Professor Tadic, the sorcerer from Harker's funeral, by the throat. *They're already here*, he realised, a jolt of panic surging through him.

He was about to step through when Evelyn appeared on the other side, blocking the way. Luke stalled, frozen with shock. "Too late," she said, then slammed the door in his face with a dull clang. Luke heard locks sliding into position. He threw himself at the metal, but it didn't give.

"Adam!"

Adam shouldered into it as well, just as the cries and screams of panic began inside the chamber.

"They're killing them!" Luke said, hurling himself again and again until the pain was too great. He might as well have been trying to knock down a concrete wall.

Adam took up the fight, but there was no way he was getting through solid metal, and he too sagged to the floor. Luke heard weapons discharging, and the shouts died down. Luke remembered what Greb had said about the Council being a place of peace. The Council members would be unarmed – completely at Dmitri's mercy.

Suddenly an idea flashed into his mind, and he extended his lightning blade. "Keep clear!" he said to

Adam. Then he drove the blade into the metal door, feeling it give as it turned molten. Heaving slowly, he cut out a circle, the gash glowing orange. Once the loop was complete he took a step back and aimed a kick at the middle. The circle of metal toppled inside with a crash.

Fear thrumming through his veins, Luke jumped into the chamber.

CHAPTER 18

The fight was already over.

Luke's eyes quickly took in the scene. Twenty or so confused Council members all herded together to one side of a huge arched chamber, their huddled shadows wavering in the light of flaming sconces set on the sandstone walls, and darkening the ancient murals and symbols smudged from centuries of dripping moisture. Energy cannons were trained on the cowering creatures by two hovering harpies. Amongst the Council members was Amelie, head of the *Canes Umbrarum*, with other werewolves, her cheek bleeding and her suit torn. An ice goblin, sharp features gleaming like a cluster of gemstones. Then what must have been a shape-shifter, face going through quick-fire transformations as it panicked.

A two-headed creature, with both heads wearing Guild of Sorcerers masks, and a small hunched reptile hybrid with scaly skin, an elongated snout, and stubby disjointed hind legs. There were a few other vampires whom Luke recognised from the wake. Plus river sprites and even a will-o'-the-wisp.

Bodies of several species, some moving weakly, others inert, lay strewn across the ground or slouched in grand chairs set at a long stone table in the centre of the room. Luke could see a variety of wounds – some looked like bites, others deep gashes. Many of the corpses were blackened and smoking, wafting the harsh aroma of singed flesh through the damp air. Luke was sickened to think the Immortals might have been responsible. Dmitri stood in the centre of the chamber. Evelyn and the others clustered together among his retinue of vampire henchmen.

"If it isn't my guinea pigs, still alive and squeaking," said Dmitri with a smile.

Luke charged at Dmitri, drawing his lightning blade. But Raziel whipped out a wing and smashed him back. Luke slid across the floor, feeling like he'd been hit by a train.

"Assume positions," said Dmitri.

Luke's head was spinning, and as he half rose on

wobbly legs, he struggled to make sense of what he was seeing. Aurora was on her knees, a stake-gun aimed at Evelyn's chest, while Evelyn gripped Aurora's Smith and Wesson, the barrel pressed against Aurora's forehead. Raziel had one of Dodger's acid vials to his lips, and with his other hand gripped Dodger's head.

Adam helped Luke to stand, a hand on his shoulder holding him steady.

"I wouldn't do anything stupid," said Dmitri. "Your friends are under instructions to kill each other if you attack me."

Luke felt sick. It was checkmate.

"How touching to see the brothers in arms," said Dmitri. "I must say, I'm surprised at you, Luke. Most people wouldn't accept such a *monster* so readily."

"Adam's no monster," said Luke. "He's more human than you'll ever be."

Dmitri feigned a hurt look. "You misunderstand," he said. "I don't mean he's literally a monster. I mean . . . he's a monster for what he did. To your family."

Luke felt Adam's grasp loosen a little. "What are you talking about?" said Luke. "My father abandoned Adam."

"Indeed he did," said Dmitri. "But that doesn't excuse what Adam did, does it?"

Luke shook his head to try and clear it.

"Oh!" said Dmitri. "I can see from your face you're confused. Didn't he tell you?"

"Please, no," begged Adam. Luke looked at his companion. Behind the mask, he saw Adam's eyes were desperate. "I wanted to, when it was time . . ."

"Tell me *what?*" asked Luke.

Dmitri reached into his jacket and took out a sheaf of papers. "I took these from Evelyn. Seems everyone's been keeping secrets from you, Luke."

Luke glanced at Evelyn. He suddenly felt small, and helpless. "What's he talking about?"

Evelyn showed no indication that she'd even heard his voice. Her finger was tight on the pistol's trigger, but Aurora showed no hint of fear.

"Allow me to enlighten you," said Dmitri. "The first entry comes from 9th November, 1848."

My birth year, thought Luke.

Dmitri read:

> *Adam has begun to behave unpredictably once more. Though I have tried to reduce his aggression through blood-letting, it shows no sign of abating. His temper comes from nowhere, like a squall in a calm ocean, but in those moments there is no*

210

reasoning with him and I fear for my safety. He beats his fists raw trying to escape his confinement. I can only judge my experiments to have been a failure, and some part of those fragments I stitched together contained a blackness, an evil even, which has survived even though the tissues and organs of which he is constituted were themselves dead . . .

The chamber was silent. *My father's journal*, thought Luke. *The missing pages.* The language was unmistakably that of Victor Frankenstein, and in his reading, Dmitri had captured the subtle inflections of his father's speech, as fresh in Luke's memory as if he had seen his father that very morning. The person he was describing didn't sound like the Adam he knew, though – the temper, and violence. Maybe he had been different in the early days of his reanimation?

"16th December," Dmitri continued.

I returned to the cabin today for the first time in almost four weeks, filled with remorse. I had been tormenting myself over whether to shoot the creature. I worried he might find his way to a habitation and hurt innocents. But I could not bring myself to do it. After all, his life was created by my hands. In the end my indecision kept me away. He is so dependent that when I returned, wracked with guilt, I expected to find his body frozen nearby. But I found his tracks leading away for some miles before losing them at a road. Some part of me was glad he may have survived the hunger and cold, but with the relief came a deep fear. Not for my own personal safety, but for the safety of nearby villagers. And, truth be told, the possibility that my work might be discovered by the authorities. I have long known that my esteemed colleagues at the university hold my experiments of the flesh to be ungodly and immoral. Perhaps they are right. But, I tell myself, the forest is huge. Adam has no concept of geography, no means of survival. As I left to hurry home, I made self-assurances that the creature would never find his way to civilisation. He will die in the forest, a confused and lonely soul not meant for this Earth.

Elizabeth is already up and walking, though the nurse-maid tells her to lie still. It looks like my son, my dear Luke, will live. His hale cries fill the valley. What man am I that such happiness and such wretched paranoia can co-exist in my heart?

Luke listened, rapt, as did the rest of the chamber. Adam, though, had shrunk away, pressing himself into the corner of the room. "What's the matter?" Luke asked. "You've told me all this before. I know my father wasn't perfect. I know what he did."

"Ah, we haven't reached the good bit yet," said Dmitri. He sifted through a few pages. "Most of this part is nauseating new-father sentiment. I won't bore you." He stopped on a page, eyes shining. "Yes, here we are. The 27th of December.

> *Today we held the funeral. Luke cries and cries for his dear mama, and from the black depths of my soul spring forth tears to match his. My dear Elizabeth is gone, and though I write those words I still cannot fathom the undeniable truth. My wife is dead. It is almost too hard to inscribe it, but I must, in order to face the consequences of my vanity and foolishness. Oh, my shattered bliss. Oh hubris!*

Dmitri paused. "Bit chest-thumping don't you think?"

Luke wanted to rip him to pieces, but his mind was full of questions. He'd never known his mother, but he knew that she died giving birth to him. So why would Victor ever blame himself? "Go on," he said.

"Very well," said Dmitri. "Where was I? Yes, hubris . . ."

I should not have been so complacent. A little over a week ago, the nursemaid reported seeing a strange, tall man at the edges of the gardens. I thought nothing of it. How could I have been so foolish? So blinded by happiness? It happened two nights later, on the 20th. I returned from dining with Dr Tulliens and his juniors down in St Eupheme du Lac to hear the baby crying. I expected to come across him in his nursemaid's arms, but instead discovered him on the ground, his cot upturned. Mystified as to how such an accident could have befallen him, I checked him for injury and found none. But my shouts to Elizabeth went unanswered. I rushed through the house, calling for the servants. Old Gerard was the first I found, my loyal butler of some five years. His back was broken at an angle so unnatural I could not fathom the force required to cause such an injury. Then the nursemaid, Annabel, her head bashed in with such violence. My breathing was terribly laboured as I climbed the stairs, clutching a poker from the fire, my condition the result not of exercise but an all-consuming terror of what I would discover there.

The bedroom. Our marital bed. She lay there, in repose, her nightclothes undisturbed. My heart begged that she was merely sleeping.

She was not. Her eyes were half open, but they saw

nothing. The signs of assault to her person were clear across her neck. Dark bruising where her murderer's hands had squeezed her life away. I touched her neck, as I had done not three hours before when I placed a necklace there, inscribed with our initials. Her cold neck...

"I could go on," said Dmitri, "but you get the gist."

"You're lying," said Luke desperately, as the room seemed to close in around him. *My mother died after she gave birth to me. A fever. That's what my father told me.*

Dmitri smiled. "You think so?"

"Master," said Adam, from the corner. "Forgive me, I beg you. I was another person then. I was so angry. I..."

Luke shook his head, unable to process. "You murdered her? My mother?"

Adam shrank back as Luke took a step towards him. "When I saw what Victor had ... what he'd left me for, I lost control. I was—"

"You lied to me," said Luke.

"*Everyone* lied to you," said Dmitri. "Your father, Harker, Evelyn. They all knew."

Luke glanced briefly at the others. At Evelyn. He didn't know how she even had the journal pages, but that didn't matter now. He turned back to Adam. His skin tingled all over, hot and itching. After all they'd been through together. At the Draper's Hall, in St. Petersburg, in the forest. "I felt *sorry* for you," spat Luke. "And all the time you were lying."

"Forgive me."

"Stop saying that!" said Luke. "You stupid *brute*. You think I can forgive you for murdering my mother?"

Adam raised his hands in front of him like a cringing child. His huge hands – the ones that had crushed the windpipe of Victor Frankenstein's wife. Luke had seen the pictures of his mother – a small, fragile woman. She wouldn't have stood a chance.

"Please, Master. Forgive—"

Luke threw himself at Adam, raining down with his fists in a frenzy. "You killed her!"

Adam didn't defend himself. Luke took a step back, breathing hard, tears streaming down his cheeks, and flashed out his lightning blade. As he brought it down, someone caught his wrist. It was Raziel. He strained to free himself, but the gargoyle held firm. He realised that Dmitri must have given the order to intervene, but in his fury he hadn't heard. Gradually his anger seeped away. Adam rolled onto his back. His mask had fallen off during the attack, and his face was bloody from Luke's blows.

"You shouldn't blame him really," said Dmitri. "As I said, he's a monster. He always was. It was your father who created him, your father who abandoned him. He admitted it in his own writing. This *tragedy* was of his own making. If you want to blame anyone, look no further than Dr Victor Frankenstein. Ms Cage – may I?" said Dmitri.

Aurora passed him the stake-launcher and he pointed it at Luke and fired.

Luke jerked in Raziel's grip, expecting an impact, but realised the stake had missed. He heard a groan and twisted around. Adam, still half-sitting on the ground, was gripping the stake, buried in his chest. His face was a mixture of pain and confusion. "Sorry to steal your thunder," said Dmitri, "but I like to take care of traitors myself."

Adam sagged back on the floor, eyes looking up at the ceiling as his breathing became weaker.

Dmitri clapped his hands together. "Now, don't despair," he said. "At least you're still alive to witness the next stage of the plan." As one, his henchmen turned their weapons on the Council members, who cowered back. *Here it comes*, thought Luke. *The massacre.*

"Please," he said. "Don't kill them."

Dmitri laughed. "Is that what you think of me,

really?" he said. "I'm not a cold-blooded killer. No, I just want a quiet word with each of them in turn. Bring them round to my point of view." As he looked at Luke, his eyes flickered black for an instant.

A cold realisation seeped through Luke. *So that's his plan. He's not going to kill the Council members at all.* "You're going to hypnotise them!"

"Why kill your enemies when you can offer them gainful employment?" said Dmitri. "If I take control of the leaders, the rest of the supernatural community will fall into line. Can you imagine what I'd do with that sort of power?"

"You're mad," said a slim, suited vampire with blonde hair, his voice quavering a little. "I'll never work for a Corrupted."

"Ah – Baines, if I'm not mistaken?" said Dmitri. "Bring him to me."

Aurora grabbed the vampire by the scruff of his neck and dragged him in front of Dmitri, who buried his teeth in Mr Baines's neck. The vampire stiffened and twitched as Dmitri sucked his blood. After a few seconds, Dmitri backed away. Mr Baines was still alive, but barely strong enough to stand. Dmitri held out a hand behind him, and one of his henchman handed him a gun. "You taste *weak*," said the Russian, and he fired a stake through Mr

Baines's chest. He screamed as he turned to crumbling ash.

Dmitri wiped his mouth. "Anyone else have something to say?" he asked brightly.

None of the other members of the Supernatural Council spoke.

"Let's begin then," said Dmitri. "Who wants to be first? And don't worry – this won't hurt at all." No one moved. "Fine," said Dmitri. He pointed at Amelie. "Bring her."

Nikolay took hold of the werewolf and pulled her in front of Dmitri. The Corrupted's eyes shone black. "You cannot resist me," he whispered, "so don't bother trying."

Amelie stared at him. "You might as well kill me too, vampire scum."

Dmitri grabbed her hair and held her face closer. "You *cannot* keep me out." He gestured to Aurora. "As you can see, I have learned to conquer even the strongest of your kind."

Luke saw a frown of confusion pass over the woman's face. Her lips moved as she began to speak, but the words were faint. Then louder: "I cannot resist you, Master."

Luke slumped in Raziel's grip. His anger had drained, leaving only helplessness. Whatever way he looked at it, they had lost. *It's over.*

CHAPTER 19

Luke glanced over to where Adam lay still. He felt nothing for him at all. Not pity, nor anger. Any warmth he'd felt for his so-called brother had turned as cold as an unlit hearth. He wondered if anything Adam said about the past was true, or if it was all lies to deceive himself and excuse what he had done. What did it matter now anyway? The past was gone, and the present was terrible enough. Adam was dead now, and that was as it should be.

Dmitri's powers were something to behold. No one was able to offer any resistance to his hypnosis. The shape-shifter's face went through several contortions as he tried to avoid the vampire's gaze, but he too succumbed after about thirty seconds. Luke could only look on, unable to break Raziel's stone hold.

He tried to think of a plan, but with his allies turning by the minute, all hope evaporated. Soon he'd be completely on his own. And then what? Would Dmitri try again to turn him, or would he simply set the rest of them on him like a pack of loyal dogs? Whatever happened, Luke promised himself he'd go out fighting.

The only chance was to exterminate Dmitri himself – to break the hold he had on the other Immortals and the Council. *But how can I even get close?*

One of the two river sprites was dragged in front of Dmitri, and at the last moment melted away, leaving the henchmen with dripping hands. She scurried as a living puddle across the floor towards the door. Dmitri clicked his fingers and one of the guards stepped up with a flame-thrower. Luke felt the blast of heat on his face as the spurting jet of fire turned the puddle to steam. The second sprite began to weep.

"Care to join your friend?" asked Dmitri.

The remaining sprite shook his head, and allowed himself to be hypnotised.

Another one down.

Then, as the river sprite stepped back to join the converted, Luke heard a roar of defiance. *It can't be.* Adam, up on his feet, stake still jutting from his chest. He staggered towards Dmitri.

The henchmen closed ranks. An electric bolt sent sparks across Adam's torso. He stumbled but didn't fall, shouldering another thug aside. A second crackle of charge hit him in the hip. Adam spun around with a cry and fell headlong at Dmitri's feet, rolling onto his front and lying still.

Dmitri leaned over the huge body, and grabbed one shoulder. "So close, old friend," he whispered. He drew a hunter's knife from behind his hip with his other hand. "You're tougher than you look."

Dmitri turned the huge man over with ease. But where Luke expected to see the stake, there was only a bloodied hole. Adam's hand flashed up, and Dmitri jerked back, looking down at his own chest, where a wooden stake was embedded just to the right side. The vampire fell to his knees, gasping.

"That is for my family," croaked Adam, his face locked in a taut grimace. Then he collapsed.

Dmitri touched the stake, as if unsure what to do. Several of his thugs rushed over to help, but Dmitri waved them off.

"Boss?" said Nikolay. "Are you okay?"

Dmitri nodded.

Luke stared at Adam's body, where he lay still. There was a kind of peacefulness in the giant's blank, open eyes. This time he knew for sure that his father's creation was no more.

Dmitri coughed up a mouthful of blood. *He's not dead. The stake must only have nicked his heart.*

As the vampire stood up, Luke sensed something odd happening around the room, almost like a shift of air pressure. Evelyn was glancing around herself, looking at the Council members and the other Immortals, frowning. Dodger too. Raziel's grip slackened. Luke looked at him, and the gargoyle gave him a solemn nod.

Then realisation dawned for Luke. *The stake must have broken his hold. They're free! Dmitri's lost control.*

Dmitri staggered towards a door, and from the panic on his face, Luke realised he knew it too. "Kill them," he spluttered. "Kill them all."

His loyal gangsters not controlled by hypnosis turned their weapons on the Supernatural Council, who, like the Immortals, were recovering, shaking their heads and muttering to one another.

"No!" cried Luke, as he saw a flame-thrower ignite.

Evelyn moved fast, gripping the barrel and twisting it upwards and back. The thug wielding it screamed as he incinerated himself. Then Dodger disappeared in a blur. Several vampire thugs fell as his tripwire upended them. Luke ducked under a grenade. It hit the wall behind and exploded into a shower of acid, filling the room with smoke as it burned into the floor.

Luke roared and ran forwards, slashing with his lightning blade, decapitating a vampire. He saw Dmitri dragging himself across the ground, and ran after him, only to come face to face with a double-barrelled shotgun. The blast lifted him off the ground and hurled him into a wall. He slid down, winded, and checked for wounds. There were none.

The thug who'd fired seemed to be fiddling with some sort of dial on the side of his weapon. Luke realised it was an energy cannon – it must have only been set for stun. *Lucky me. Unlucky him.* He picked himself up, drove a flying knee into the attacker's cranium, then picked up the weapon himself. He rolled the dial to max, just in time to take out one of the harpies. She hit the ceiling with a dull splat, stuck there for a moment, then fell to the ground in several pieces.

Carnage all around him. He saw Dmitri sucking at the throat of one of his own men, who twitched and struggled weakly. *He's recovering.* Aurora ducked under a hook from Nikolay, then delivered two jabs and an uppercut which sent the ogre staggering away. A sorcerer teleported behind a vampire then gripped the top of his head. A few muttered words and the vampire shrivelled like a human raisin, instantly mummified. *That's one move BIOS could never give me.* Raziel spun in the air with a harpy on his back, and crashed into a wall. With a roar he pushed back, crushing her against the opposite wall. Her wings went limp as she crumpled on the ground. Greb was smashing a henchman's head repeatedly into the door. More grenades threw billows of smoke across the room.

We're winning, thought Luke. *But it's not over.*

Evelyn fell against him, twirling her fighting staff.

"I think I owe you an apology," she said.

"I'll settle for you not trying to kill me," Luke replied. "It's good to have you back."

She felled a gangster with a thrusting jab to the temple. "Where's Dmitri?" she asked.

Luke looked again for the Corrupted, but he was gone. A shape was moving through the door.

"After him!" Luke said.

He and Evelyn crossed the room, stepping over fallen bodies. They found Aurora, fists bloody, standing over Nikolay. The ogre wasn't quite dead, but he wouldn't be winning any beauty contests for a while. "Go!" said the werewolf. "We can finish up here."

Evelyn and Luke plunged through the doorway.

Dmitri was easy to track – a trail of red spatters on

the floor, bloody handprints on the walls where he'd steadied himself. *He's injured, but not mortally. We can't let him escape.*

They splashed through silt and filthy water, climbing a number of metal ladders to more elevated shafts. Luke had no idea where they were going, or if Dmitri did either, but they were getting closer to the surface all the time. Then the tracks stopped in the middle of a tunnel.

Evelyn pointed upwards, to an open wooden hatch. Luke made out a peeling plaster ceiling above. There was no ladder.

Luke jumped up and grabbed the lip, heaving himself into a room filled with shelves, stacked wooden chairs, and other junk. It looked like something from Victorian times. A storage room of some sort, without any light at all. *A basement.* A narrow stone staircase was the only entry point from above. There was no sign of Dmitri. Luke reached down and seized Evelyn's outstretched hand, hauling her up alongside him.

"I guess he went that way," said Luke, nodding to the stairs. He ran over, but Evelyn called him back. She grabbed one of the chairs and smashed it against the wall, leaving her holding the two legs. "We need weapons."

"Good thinking." Luke extended his lightning blade,

and made short work of sharpening the lengths of wood into charred stakes. He promised himself he wouldn't miss the target like Adam had.

They crept up the stairs, then through another door into a wide corridor with a concrete floor, tiled walls and a musty smell. There was more blood spattered on the floor, but less volume. *He's healing already . . .*

The passage led to another set of stairs, and when they emerged above it was into much grander surroundings. A hall with high ceilings, brocade curtains and a luxurious red carpet. A sign with arrows read "Westminster Hall" and "Main Lobby". There were railings with ropes suspended between them, blocking access to certain doors. The whole place was dimly lit by chandeliers.

"We're in the Houses of Parliament!" said Evelyn, and her voice echoed off the walls.

The blood was harder to spot on the carpet, but Luke saw a smear on a wall, where an arrow pointed to "The Clock Tower" through a doorway. A single chair stood against the wall, and beside it on a table was a steaming mug.

"Someone was here," said Luke.

Evelyn's eyes widened as a man launched himself through the door towards them. He was at least sixty, red-faced, and dressed in a white ruff collar, padded red frock coat, and a black hat. *A beefeater!* But it was the man's halberd that caught Luke's attention. He ducked and the blade thumped into the wall.

The old man jerked it free, then advanced on them.

"He's been hypnotised!" said Luke. "Don't hurt him."

The blade whistled back and forth as the beefeater swung wildly and grunted. Evelyn darted past, grabbed the edge of a hanging curtain and tore it free. She threw it over the man's head, then tripped him up. They left him squirming on the ground.

The staircase up to the Clock Tower was a spiral. Looking up, Luke heard shuffling footsteps and caught sight of Dmitri leaning over. When the vampire saw him below, he vaulted onto the bannister, and pounced across the drop to the next level with incredible agility. Then he jumped back the other way. He was already way above them, getting further out of reach by the second.

Luke shook off his satchel and drew out the grapple gun. It had a range of fifty metres, but he had no idea how high the clock tower was. "Grab on to me," he said to Evelyn.

"Will this thing hold us both?" she asked.

Luke fired and the cable whistled out. With an echoing clang, the grapple snagged on a railing fifty metres up.

"Let's see," he said, and set the gun to retract. His feet left the floor and they shot into the air, passing turns and turns of the staircase in a blur. In a matter of seconds, Luke and Evelyn were clambering onto stairs near the top. Dmitri was nowhere to be seen.

They continued on foot. At the top of the stairs, a doorway opened into a cavernous cold space filled with industrial mechanisms blocked off by railings. The four walls were each dominated by a luminous white clock face twenty feet high and marked with Roman numerals. It was a few minutes short of seven pm.

"Dmitri must have gone up further," said Evelyn.

They climbed again through another door labelled "Bell Tower".

The stairs narrowed into a tighter spiral, with arched windows giving views of the London skyline in all directions. As they climbed, Luke's memory snagged on a moment from his youth. He had been in London with his father, and they had paused outside Westminster Palace to marvel at the tower being built. The scaffolding had seemed to soar, higher than anything else around, the workmen like ants scurrying across the joists and beams.

Now the tower was one of many. Skyscrapers across the river rose at least as high.

They reached the belfry, and paused in the doorway. Luke gasped at the size of Big Ben, the brass bell suspended from riveted steel girders above them. There were sets of stairs to give access and a giant cantilevered hammer poised to strike. He looked down, and wished he hadn't.

Further doors, cordoned off, were visible above. Had Dmitri climbed higher still? If so, where was he running to? *There's no way out.*

As soon as Luke took a step into the tower, he sensed a shadow.

By the time he looked up it was too late.

CHAPTER 20

Dmitri swiped him across the face and Luke fell hard against the wall. He saw Evelyn kicked in the gut and dropped to the floor. Dmitri picked up her stake, spun it in his hand so the tip was downward.

No . . .

The Corrupted vampire jammed the stake through Evelyn's thigh, and she screamed.

"I'll feast on your life when I'm ready, Ms Harker," said Dmitri.

Groggy, Luke lifted his fingers to touch his cheek and they came away bloody. *Just a flesh wound.* Dmitri pounced and Luke raised the stake still clutched in his hand. But the vampire caught Luke's forearm and squeezed. The electric current from his nail implants shot up Luke's arm, and he dropped the stake. Dmitri jammed his other fist into Luke's chest, smashing him against the massive bell. Luke fell to his knees, lungs unable to find air.

Dmitri grabbed his hair, and pulled him to his feet. Luke gripped the vampire's wrist, yanked it free with a clump of his own hair. He ignored the pain and threw up his feet, hooking his ankles around the back of Dmitri's neck. It was a move he'd practised with Evelyn in the dojo a hundred times – the flying armbar. He pulled hard on Dmitri's arm, hanging upside-down, flexing the elbow over his leg until he fell the tendons give, then the bone.

Dmitri roared and lifted Luke higher, even on his broken arm. Luke held on as the vampire carried him in staggering steps, then swung him head-first into the bell's rim. The metal implants on his skull made a dull clang, and Luke fell, collapsing semi-conscious to the ground. He saw Dmitri clutching his elbow, where a shard of bone was jutting through the skin. Then the vampire grinned. Luke saw the bone reset, the skin heal over, in less than five seconds.

"Impressive, isn't it?" said Dmitri. "Amazing what you can achieve with a good diet."

"A cannibal diet," said Luke.

He shot out his lightning blade, but Dmitri bobbed and rabbit-punched his elbow, deflecting the blow. The hissing blade slashed across Big Ben, throwing off sparks and scarring the metal. Dmitri lifted his hand, and the nail implants crackled. He drove them into Luke's right shoulder, sending wave after wave of electric current deep into his implants. Luke screamed, unable to fight back as the agony burned through his arm. The stink of burning flesh filled his nose.

"Stings a bit, I imagine," said Dmitri, his face illuminated by the flashing electricity.

He drew back his arm and Luke flopped to the floor. He felt utterly drained. His whole body throbbed. The lightning blade had withdrawn, and when he tried to summon it again, he couldn't even feel his arm.

Paralysed.

Evelyn was still on the ground, breathing but lying still.

Dmitri looked from one to the other, as if deciding whom to finish off first. His eyes settled on Luke. "You know, there's a kind of justice in this," he said. "You can pay for your father's sins."

He stooped beside Luke, who raised his left arm to try to ward off the vampire. Dmitri batted it easily aside. "Even with all your clever additions, I don't think you can live without blood in your veins. Take comfort, Luke. Your death is not a waste."

He clamped his teeth into Luke's throat. Luke felt the fangs sink into his flesh easily, and after the initial pain, there was nothing but a sensation of emptying – of coldness spreading across his skin. He had no fight left. *I'm dying. Bleeding out like a slaughtered animal.*

Dmitri jerked and the fangs withdrew suddenly. Through a sudden wave of pain, Luke saw the vampire's face, puzzled. Then the end of a bloody chair leg broke through the front of his shirt, right above his heart.

Evelyn peered over his shoulder. "Chest pains?" she said.

Dmitri reached for the stake, but already the skin across his hands and face was blackening, as if his blood had turned to ink. His eyes blackened too, then black tears began to leak from the corners. The arm holding Luke down shrivelled, thinner and thinner, until it looked like a charred branch. Then all its strength and weight vanished as it disintegrated into ash. Dmitri fell backwards and, mouth splitting open in a wail, the flesh of his face shrank away to reveal a black skull, jaws just moving as if trying to speak from the grave. Evelyn grabbed the skull and tugged. It crumbled in her hands.

She flopped against the bell beside Luke.

"Are you still with it?" she said. Her thigh was bleeding heavily. *She must have pulled out the stake.*

Luke, clutching his neck, looked at the pile of ash where their enemy had been standing a few seconds ago. "Never better," he said weakly.

"Don't worry," she said. "Your body produces an enzyme that fights off vampiric infection."

"That's good to know," said Luke, smiling. "Wouldn't want to turn into a bloodsucker, would I?"

"Watch it!" said Evelyn, giving him a shove.

When they arrived back underground, the Immortals seemed to have everything under control. Those of Dmitri's henchmen who were still breathing had been tied up with rope, and stood sullenly against a wall. The Council members were sitting down, deep in discussion, while others were clearing bodies, or bits of them. Everyone turned to look as they entered the room.

"Dmitri is dead," said Luke. "Evelyn staked him."

His friend grinned. "Team effort."

Dodger took off his hat and held it over his chest. "About the whole hunting-you-down thing – my humblest regrets."

Luke smiled. "I'm lucky you're so bad at it," he replied.

Raziel bowed his head. "Master, forgive me. I will forever be ashamed I did not have the strength to withstand the vampire."

"Some things aren't a case of strength," said Luke. "Don't worry about it. Sorry about the machine-gun."

Aurora lifted her chin. "Yeah. Sorry, kid. Not myself there for a while."

Luke saw a couple of werewolves picking up Adam's body by the arms and legs. The bronze mask was balanced on his chest.

"Wait," he said, walking over. He still felt a bit light-headed from the blood loss. "Leave him."

The werewolves laid Adam down again, and Luke knelt beside the giant. His scarred features looked peaceful at last. Luke swallowed, letting the room get on with things without him. He didn't care if anyone was watching.

It could all have been so different. What if Victor had never abandoned Adam? What if he'd tried harder to help his creation control his rage at the beginning? They might have grown up together. Adam might have been happy.

I would have had a mother . . .

If. Might. Could. You could replay half your life in possibilities, but you had to play the cards fate dealt.

"You shouldn't blame yourself," said Aurora. "He had a curse hanging over him from the start."

A curse of my father's making, thought Luke. *He even said as much in his journal.*

Reaching out, Luke replaced the bronze mask. "Farewell, brother," he whispered. "Be at peace." As he turned, he saw Evelyn watching him.

"I'm sorry I sent him away," she said.

"He was a spy," said Luke sadly. "You were right not to trust him."

"That's not the point," she said. She crouched too. "We could bury him at Southwark – if that's what you want?"

Luke nodded. "Even though he killed my mother, Dmitri was right about one thing. It's my father who was to blame."

"Luke, you shouldn't say that. Victor was a good man."

"And even good people make mistakes," said Luke. "I wanted to think my dad was perfect, but no one is. He was always consumed in his work, but to lose perspective that much – to play God. I think that's one of the reasons he started the Immortals. To make amends."

"I think you're right," said Evelyn.

"How long did you have those papers about Adam?" Luke asked.

"Only since the funeral," said Evelyn. "My father had them. He wanted to tell you. I wanted to."

Luke looked up at his friend. "I understand."

Aurora cleared her throat behind them. "I think we're done here," she said. "What shall we do with the prisoners?"

Luke expected Evelyn to answer, but then he realised that Evelyn was looking at him. All the Supernatural Council were.

"Er . . . I suppose we question them," said Luke. "Try to work out who was working for Dmitri under hypnosis. If they were, free them."

"And if not?" asked Raziel.

"Let the Council decide," said Luke.

Several heads around the gathering nodded and began dark muttering. Dodger hopped up onto the table, raising his hands for silence. "Hang on a minute. There's one more . . . erm . . . item on the agenda."

"Yes?" said Amelie, looking at him distastefully from the head of the table.

"Well, I just think it needs to be raised . . . well, that the Immortals saved your sorry skins *again*. All well and good for you lot to talk about disbanding us, but the fact remains that you'd all be singing from the same vampire hymn-sheet if it weren't for Luke here. You should be thanking us."

Several of the Council members were glaring coldly at Dodger.

"I believe this ... individual ... has a point," said Greb the sewer troll, at last.

Not everyone looked convinced, so Luke ushered Dodger down from the table. "What Dodger is saying," he said, "is that we want to work *with* you, not against you. My father set up the Immortals to defend innocent life. He gave his own life to protect London. Sometimes we need to act, rather than just talk. We've made mistakes, I know, but with your help and your combined knowledge, we can make the world safer."

The others came to stand beside him, so they were facing the Council.

Evelyn spoke up. "Jonathan Harker was a great believer in cooperation – that's why he kept the Immortals going even after Victor Frankenstein had passed on. It would honour his memory if we worked together with you."

Amelie spoke to a sorcerer beside her in a whisper, then to an elderly vampire on her other side. She stood up.

"We agree with what you're both saying. And for that reason, we would like to offer you *all* a place on the Supernatural Council. Many of our members feel threatened by your activities, but recognise your merits. From this day forward, the Immortals and Council will work as one."

Luke looked at his friends. Raziel bowed, Dodger clapped his hands, and Aurora gave the sparest of nods. Evelyn was smiling.

"We still have one problem though," said the elderly vampire. "The journalist. We must do everything in our power to throw her off the scent."

Luke tried not to let his face betray any emotion. He'd forgotten about Amy Short, but she'd still be waiting back at the base.

"Don't worry about her," he said. "We've got everything completely under control."

CHAPTER 21

"I'm publishing," declared Amy Short, folding her arms. "Tomorrow. And there's nothing you can do or say that will stop me."

Completely under control, Luke repeated to himself.

They were back under the cathedral at Southwark, and so far the conversation wasn't going brilliantly.

"No. You're. Not," said Dodger.

"Ever heard of freedom of the press?" asked Amy.

"Have you ever heard of potassium cyanide?" said Dodger, waving a vial at her.

"I'm not scared of you," said Amy. She began to mutter about censorship, and murder threats, until Luke cut in.

"Let her go," he said.

"*What?*" said Dodger and Amy at the same time.

"I say we let her go," said Luke.

"Thank you," said Amy. "At least someone here sees sense."

"But ..." said Luke. "I really don't think you should go publishing any silly stories."

"Or what? You'll set the poisoner on me?"

"No," said Luke. "We're not murderers. Like it or not, we've sworn to protect humans from supernatural forces. But to do that, we have to protect our secrets. And if that means hacking your computers and deleting all your files, if it means sabotaging the print presses, or burning down the odd office, then that's fair game."

"You wouldn't! You *couldn't*!"

Aurora laughed. "Amy, sweetheart. We could do that before breakfast."

"And," said Evelyn, "if you start talking about living gargoyles, vampires and werewolves, your employers at *The Times* will have you out of the door faster than even Dodger here can run. I've gone through your files. You really haven't got a lot."

Amy reddened. "But—"

"Look," said Luke. "Your readers don't want to know the truth, because most of them wouldn't be able to accept it anyway. Think about it. People have tried to tell the world about our folk before. And it's never worked. The rumours never take hold."

"Yes, but—"

"So let's cut a deal. We'll feed you information when we can. We come across criminals all the time. Instead of being the crazy lady who got fired from *The Times*, you could be the cutting edge crime correspondent with all the scoops."

He saw Amy's face relax as she pondered his offer.

"Start with Big Ben," Luke said. "I heard there was an incident there last night. Someone got in, vandalised the bell. That's a serious security breach at the Houses of Parliament. Good story, right?"

"I'll need more than that," said Amy.

"How about bloodstains everywhere?"

Amy smiled, despite herself. "Okay," she said. "You'd better not be lying."

"So do we have your word you won't mention anything about this place?" asked Evelyn.

"Do I have yours that no one will kill me?"

Luke looked at everyone. Raziel and Aurora nodded, and Evelyn said, "Of course we won't."

Dodger sulked with his arms folded.

"Dodger?" said Luke.

"I won't kill her," he said. "Promise."

Luke escorted Amy Short to the elevator, and waved her goodbye.

When he turned back into the room, he shrugged. "You think we can trust her?" he said.

Dodger unfolded his arms and held up a hand with his fingers crossed. "Never trust anyone," he said.

"Let's use BIOS to hack the computers anyway," said Evelyn. "Monitor all her electronic communications and writing."

"I can trail her movements," said Aurora.

"I'll bug her apartment," said Dodger.

"And I'll watch for anything unusual outside," said Raziel.

Luke grinned to see the Immortals getting on with things as normal. Despite everything, they were still a team. But things were moving too fast. Could they really trust Amy to keep her mouth shut?

"This place is compromised," he said. "We need to find a new base, at least for a while."

Evelyn, already heading to a computer terminal, paused. "You may be right. I think I know a place where we can hole up."

Two days later, Luke was standing on a barren clifftop, looking out over a choppy, gunmetal sea. The buffeting wind snatched at his clothes, and those of the others. Only Raziel was completely still, perched like a statue. The helicopter stood a few hundred metres away.

Aurora and Dodger removed their hats as Evelyn

tipped the urn and scattered her father's ashes onto the jagged rocks below, then turned back inland. Set on the sloping hillside was a small cottage, its roof collapsed, and walls crumbling. Aside from that, the wild landscape of Iona was empty.

"Dad loved it here," Evelyn said. "We used to come every summer."

"It's supposed to be summer now, isn't it?" said Dodger, shivering.

Luke savoured the rugged beauty. He knew Evelyn's memories of this place weren't entirely happy. It was here, on Iona – the small island off the coast of Scotland – in the summer of 1842, that Dracula's sisters had come to take their revenge. To pay back Jonathan Harker for the stake he and Van Helsing had driven through Count Dracula's heart. Evelyn's mother and baby brother had been killed. The sisters had spared her father, and her, but had cursed them both. But fate moved in strange ways. If it weren't for Dracula's sisters, Evelyn would have likely lived a normal life. Luke would never have met her. Perhaps the Immortals would never have existed.

If. Might. Could.

Death closed avenues, but it opened new ones.

"I kind of like it," said Aurora. "Quiet."

Dodger shot her a sideways look. "You would. You haven't got any friends."

Aurora growled.

"You want to tell them?" asked Evelyn.

"Tell us what?" asked Aurora.

Luke smiled. "Evelyn and I have been talking," he said. "Her family own all the land here for several miles. We could build a base here and no one would ever bother us."

"For how long?" asked Dodger. "I'm pretty sure Wong's doesn't deliver this far from the West End."

"As long as necessary," said Luke.

"That supposed to be a straight answer?" said Dodger. "I need to know how many pairs of woolly long johns to pack."

"I think it's a good idea," said Raziel. Of all of them, he looked the most at home in the bare rocky surroundings.

"Let's get out of this wind," said Aurora. She began to walk towards the helicopter.

Luke remained for a moment with Evelyn, watching the others follow Aurora. "Dodger will come round," Evelyn said. "He likes to pretend he doesn't need us, but it's just an act."

"We all need somebody," said Luke. "It's what makes

us people." He opened his palm, and looked at the pendant in the middle with his parents' initials. He'd taken it from Adam's body before they cremated it back at the base. "Adam just wanted a family."

"You'll miss him, won't you?" said Evelyn.

"I don't know if that's true," said Luke. "But I would have liked to know him better. And I can't help thinking . . . what if things had been different. What if my dad hadn't abandoned—"

"You shouldn't think like that," said Evelyn. "Actions have consequences you can't predict. If Adam hadn't been created, maybe your father would never have met mine, and we'd never have become friends, or joined the Immortals."

"And you wouldn't have tried to hunt me down and kill me in a Russian forest," said Luke. He glanced at Evelyn, who smiled back.

"I thought we'd dealt with that," she said.

"I'm still processing," said Luke.

"Seriously, though," said Evelyn. "All I'm saying is that you can't pinpoint one event and blame it for everything that came after. Life doesn't work like that. It's a continuum. Once you've lived for two centuries, maybe you'll appreciate that."

Luke hooked the chain over his own neck, and let the

pendant hang against his chest. Waves crashed into the base of the cliffs, hurling spray. "Let's go," he said.

They turned from the seascape, and headed after the others. On the way, Evelyn kept looking towards the house.

"Are you sure about this?" he asked. "I mean, here?"

"It's been nearly two hundred years," said Evelyn cheerfully. "Time to move on."

Luke could tell she was putting on a brave face.

His phone beeped as they neared the helicopter, and he read a message.

"Look sharp," he told the others. "We've got a problem."

"Haven't we always?" said Dodger.

"What is it?" asked Aurora.

"Professor Tadic," said Luke. "He says the Library archives were broken into last night. A spell book has been stolen. He's asking for our help."

"That guy creeps me out," said Dodger. "His eyes follow you around the room. Shall we tell him to get lost?"

Everyone looked at him.

"You lot are so bloomin' worthy," said Dodger.

Evelyn clambered into the pilot's seat ahead of Luke. "I'm flying," she said.

Luke climbed in beside her. "Fine by me," he said, before adding quietly, "You need the practice."

With the ear-defenders already on, Evelyn didn't hear him – or she chose not to. Luke grinned as they climbed over the scrubby moorland and swung away over the sea.